THE PLOT TO GET CLOUSEAU . . .

"All this? To get one cop?" Cairo Fred did not understand. "He can't be that good."

"Good!" Dreyfus cackled. "No. Clouseau is not good. He is terrible! The worst! He is unlike any man, anywhere, ever! You cannot even talk about him the way you talk about other men. And you can thank God that there is only one of him. Compared to a dozen Clouseaus, the Doomsday Machine would be a water pistol! Mark my word . . . It will take all the ingenuity of the Great Powers with all their trained assassins and all of their sophisticated murder weapons to eliminate Clouseau! And even then there is a chance that they might fail."

Even Hindu Harry was impressed. Clouseau, he conceded, did not sound human.

"Human?" laughed Dreyfus. He was beginning to throw a fit. "That is what I've been trying to tell you! Of course he is not human!"

Peter Sellers

in

Blake Edwards'

THE PINK PANTHER
STRIKES AGAIN

Starring Herbert Lom
with Colin Blakely
and Leonard Rossiter
Lesley-Anne Down

Animation by **Richard Williams Studio**

Music by **Henry Mancini**

"Come to Me" Sung by **Tom Jones**

Associate Producer **Tony Adams**

Screenplay by **Frank Waldman and Blake Edwards**

Produced and Directed by **Blake Edwards**

United Artists
A Transamerica Company

BLAKE EDWARDS'

THE PINK PANTHER STRIKES AGAIN

©U.A.C.—GEOFFREY

by Frank Waldman

Adapted from the screenplay by

Frank Waldman
and Blake Edwards

BALLANTINE BOOKS • NEW YORK

All Rights Reserved. Published in the United States by Ballantine Books, a division of Random House, Inc., New York, and simultaneously in Canada by Ballantine Books of Canada, Ltd., Toronto, Canada.

ISBN 0-345-27055-X

Manufactured in the United States of America

First Edition: December 1976

First Special Printing: January 1977

1

For Dr. Claude Duval, resident psychiatrist at France's State Mental Health Facility for the Criminally Insane, success in the most difficult case of a brilliant medical career was but a matter of hours away. Or, to be exact, two hours and thirty-one minutes. A modest man, Dr. Duval could practically taste the Nobel prize that must assuredly be his.

Eighteen months ago, a deranged wreck of a man, former respected Chief Inspector in the Sûreté, had been delivered into his care. Dr. Duval repressed a slight shudder as he recalled his first sight of Charles Dreyfus. He could still see the man's foam-flecked lips contorted in a perpetual snarl, the wildly rolling eyes, still hear the animal-like curses and snarls that could be elicited by the mere mention of the name *Clouseau*.

Dr. Duval stood at his office window and gazed with satisfaction over the manicured grounds of the institution he had served for close to twenty years. Inmates and attendants strolled the well-kept lawns or sprawled in the comfortable wicker furniture placed about the grounds. Swans paddling in the artificial lake added a sense of tranquillity to the surroundings.

The ten-foot-high security wall encircling the establishment was concealed by shrubbery. Only the building housing the dangerous patients had bars on its windows. If one had to endure madness, where better than at "Crazy Acres," as the facility was popularly known throughout the region?

Dr. Duval turned from the window. A frown crossed his unpleasant, rather gross features as he reviewed past failures with the patient Dreyfus. (Dr.

1

Duval abhorred the word inmate and never permitted its use in regard to those unfortunates placed under his care. Dr. Duval considered himself a kindly man. Madame Duval and the children might have told a different story.)

With former Chief Inspector Dreyfus, electrotherapy had been a complete failure. Electric shock treatment had had no effect on the man. Saline baths had been tried with a similar lack of results. Massage, confinement, group therapy—all had been attempted and discarded. Only when Dr. Duval, in desperation, had invented the celebrated Clouseau doll had poor, shattered Charles Dreyfus begun the long, torturous climb back to normalcy.

Dr. Duval crossed to his closet, opened the door, and took out the stuffed dummy. It was nearly life-size and a remarkable likeness of Jacques Clouseau had been painted in detail on the dummy's face. Dr. Duval could still remember his patient's words when he first say the dummy.

"That goddamned dummy looks like that goddamned dummy!" the unfortunate Dreyfus had screamed; after which he had struck the dummy with his clenched fist time and again, until he was emotionally drained and had to be returned to his room.

But thereafter, for the better part of a year, Dreyfus had begun to look forward to his therapy sessions with his psychiatrist. The opportunity to "beat the shit out of Clouseau" was the only thing that had kept him going. So he vented his rage and frustration on the Clouseau dummy-doll, which was the image of the man whose idiosyncracies and maddening habits had driven him over the brink of insanity, and was thus able to begin the long climb back to stability and mental health. In the intervening months, the dummy had taken a fearful beating. Time and again the stuffing had been beaten out of it, only to be replaced for the next session. The painted mouth had been cracked repeatedly; the eyes were long since gone.

But the transference of rage from the unattainable Clouseau outside the walls to the lifelike dummy

2

within reach of Dreyfus's flailing fists had brought about the miracle. Dreyfus's knuckles were as completely healed as his mind. Soon Dr. Duval would tell his favorite patient about the sanity hearing that was to take place that afternoon. It was the only thing standing between Dreyfus and release from "Crazy Acres," release that had once been considered beyond the realm of possibility.

Two muscular male attendants in hospital whites ushered in the patient. The attendants withdrew. Dr. Duval eyed the former Chief Inspector of Police. Dreyfus looked well. He was neatly dressed. His hair was carefully combed. He had shaved himself without so much as a nick or scratch. Also his nails were unbitten.

"Good morning, Charles," said the doctor, smiling.

"Good morning," beamed the patient. "Should I adopt the reclining posture?" Dreyfus indicated the psychiatrist's couch.

Dr. Duval smiled. "Only if you wish to."

Dreyfus sank into a leather wing chair and crossed his legs comfortably. "I don't feel it is necessary. In fact, if I were you, I would pronounce me cured. Does that make sense?"

"Indeed it does." Dr. Duval opened a cigarette box on the desk and offered it to Dreyfus, who shook his head.

"I'm surprised at you, Doctor," he chided.

"Of course. I forgot. You quit. Forgive me, my dear fellow."

Dreyfus waved his hand. "Three months ago." He chuckled. "There was a time your forgetfulness would have made me feel rejected."

"But not now?" Dr. Duval waited for the answer that would reveal so much.

"Well." Dreyfus shrugged. "A little rejected perhaps. If I hadn't realized you did it intentionally."

"And why would I do that?"

"A test? For a patient you consider to be rehabilitated?" surmised Dreyfus.

Dr. Duval's eyes roved the office, seeking the

likeliest spot for his Nobel prize. "Not so long ago an obvious trick like that would have sent you into a towering rage."

Former Chief Inspector Dreyfus smiled fondly at the battered dummy. "And poor old Clouseau would have submitted to another massacre. It's a miracle you were able to keep putting him back together." Dreyfus patted the dummy fondly. "Let alone me. Poor old Clouseau. And not so long ago I couldn't speak his name . . . hear his name . . . without losing control."

"You were capable of killing Clouseau," the psychiatrist reminded.

"Yes." Dreyfus looked thoughtful. "I was a sick man, wasn't I? We've come a long way."

Dr. Duval appeared to be doodling idly on his pad. In reality he was drawing pictures of nurses' breasts. "And you're not even a little bit bothered now when you think of Clouseau?"

Dreyfus shook his head. "Not even a little bit. Do you believe me? I could be lying. You're a good psychiatrist, but I might be a better liar."

"For your sake, I hope not." The psychiatrist switched from breasts to buttocks. "Sooner or later you'd run into Clouseau and then . . . back inside here for life. No more chances for another sanity hearing."

Dreyfus looked properly grave. "I know. Day after day, coming here, watching you chain-smoke yourself into an early grave, knowing that on certain mornings you will be particularly morose and testy because you have had another fight with your wife—like this morning."

Dr. Duval was taken aback. "How do you know that?"

"The only time you doodle," observed Dreyfus, his police training asserting itself, "is when you fight with your wife."

Dr. Duval fenced. "Why does it have to be my wife?"

4

Dreyfus remained unshaken, sure of himself. "Your mistress then."

"I keep forgetting you were Chief Inspector in the Sûreté." The analyst smiled.

"And will be again," promised Dreyfus.

Dr. Duval eyed him narrowly. "But Clouseau is the Chief Inspector."

"Until a better man comes along," Dreyfus conceded.

"I think he has." Dr. Duval got up from behind his desk to shake hands with his about-to-be-former patient. "You might as well begin packing. By the way, there is a sanity hearing for you this afternoon. Purely a formality in your case. If all goes the way I expect it to, you will be out of here tomorrow."

Dreyfus stood up and shook his benefactor's hand. "As you can see, I am in complete control. Although I have lived for this day, my hand does not tremble. Nor does my voice break. Nor is there the trace of a tear in my eye. You know something, Doctor? You're a hell of a psychiatrist!"

Even as the happy Dreyfus was marching back to his room to get out his valise, an official-looking black Citroën was driving onto the hospital grounds. The Citroën spelled trouble for Dreyfus. Beside the police detective-driver sat Chief Inspector Jacques Clouseau.

"I shall not be too long." Clouseau took out a Gauloise and pushed in the dashboard cigarette lighter. "A brief but pleasant chat . . . a few words of encouragement to poor old Dreyfus."

"Does he know you are coming?" queried the driver, François.

Clouseau shook his head. "I want it to be a surprise." He stared at the cigarette lighter in his hand and said, "Merde." The filament part of the lighter was still stuck in the dashboard and was beginning to overheat. "It appears that you have a defective lighter."

The driver skillfully avoided an inmate in a

wheelchair. "It's supposed to pop out automatically when it reaches a specific temperature."

"And exactly what is this specific temperature?" Clouseau cross-examined his subordinate. The driver admitted that he had no idea.

Clouseau continued his relentless grilling. "You should have checked with the factory. It is obvious your poop-out"—mispronouncing the word—"lighter has reached the specific temperature and is refusing to poop out."

He took a screwdriver from the glove compartment. "It is also obvious you have forgotten the first rule of the car owner: Know your automobile."

"It is not my automobile," the driver objected. "It is your automobile."

Clouseau impatiently jabbed the screwdriver into the smoke-filled lighter hole. Instantly there was a great flash of light followed by an explosion under the hood. Great clouds of yellow smoke billowed up from the engine. Clouseau got out of the stalled auto.

"You also appear to have a defective electrical system," he said calmly and trotted off up one of the pretty little paths criss-crossing the hospital grounds.

Clouseau hummed as he hurried along. It was a beautiful day, was it not? And was he not embarked on a mission of kindness? Bringing comfort and encouragement to a poor old madman with whom he had served, shoulder to shoulder, in the famed Paris Sûreté? Clouseau found himself skirting the placid lake. I wonder, he mused, if they call this Lake Placid?

An inmate wearing an American Indian headdress stood off to one side shooting rubber-suction-tipped arrows at a toy target. In passing, Clouseau raised two fingers in the Indian peace sign. In response the inmate raised his middle finger in the internationally known up-yours sign. Clouseau hurried on his way.

He was crossing an expanse of lawn. Something caught his eye. Clouseau stopped. Someone had left a croquet mallet in the grass beside two croquet balls.

Clouseau picked up the mallet idly, positioned himself over the two balls, planted a foot on the nearest ball and swung. The second ball zoomed off like a shell fired from a howitzer, caromed off a tree, disappeared over a slight rise, and caught Charles Dreyfus squarely in the back of the head. Dreyfus instantly stopped walking to his sanity hearing and toppled into the lake.

2

The first thing Clouseau saw when he topped the rise was a man thrashing about in the lily pads and muttering cries for help. Surprisingly, the man in the lake bore a remarkable resemblance to Charles Dreyfus. Clouseau rushed to the water's edge, determined to perform a heroic rescue. By now Dreyfus's kicking and splashing was beginning to unnerve the swans.

When Clouseau realized the man in the water was too far from shore to be seized by the hand, he alertly held out the mallet.

"Here!" Clouseau shouted. "Grab on and I'll have you out on dry land in less time than it takes to say . . . *merde!*"

Dreyfus, having seized the head of the mallet, saw it come off the shaft as he fell back into the lake.

Clouseau yelled encouragement. "Tread water! I have not given up!" He cast about frantically for a branch, a pole . . . anything.

"Go away!" shouted Dreyfus. "For God's sake, let me drown in peace!"

Clouseau snatched up a gardener's rake and held it out to Dreyfus, who instinctively grabbed hold. Clouseau pulled the mud-spattered victim onto dry ground. Water ran off of Dreyfus's clothing. Duck feathers and lily pads festooned his hair. Dreyfus took one look at his rescuer, saw it was the hated Clouseau, and promptly fainted.

The alert Clouseau instantly leaped astride Dreyfus and started applying mouth-to-mouth resuscitation. Two female inmates, Psycho Sarah and Manic Mamie, came wandering down the path innocently pulling the wings off butterflies.

"Don't look, Mamie!" Sarah clapped her huge hands over her friend's eyes, then angrily bashed Clouseau over the head with her purse. "Pervert!" she yelled in a voice that sounded like the cry of a freeze-dried loon.

Sarah struggled to see. "Dirty old men." She grinned at Clouseau and Dreyfus as Mamie yanked her away by the ear. "I'm in Ward C."

Dreyfus struggled to sit up.

"There is no need to thank me," Clouseau assured him. "I did nothing any other self-effacing hero would not have done."

Dreyfus tried to get his eyes to focus. "Someone . . . I was hit on the head with something."

Clouseau examined Dreyfus's skull. "Ah." He confirmed his findings. "You have received the large beump."

"Beump?" repeated Dreyfus.

"What?" asked Clouseau.

"You said beump," Dreyfus accused.

"I know." Clouseau tried to be placating. "Such a beump could be serious. You could have a concussion. Or even a fracture of the skull. In any event, you should not get up."

Dreyfus struggled weakly to get away from his tormentor. "I'm fine. Never better. Just a little shaky. Probably the shock of seeing you again . . . here . . . today, of all days."

Clouseau waved disarmingly. Perhaps he might say a few words on Dreyfus's behalf to the Sanity Commission Review Board? "As we both know," Clouseau noted, "I am not without influence."

The thought of Clouseau interceding on his behalf at the sanity hearing was too much for Dreyfus. He managed to get up and scuttle to a bench, trying to get as far from Clouseau as he could. Dreyfus sat wringing his hands and moaning to himself. His left eye began to twitch alarmingly.

"Yes," Clouseau intoned, "I have become a rather important official in the department since you went crazy. We have made several important changes. You would hardly recognize the old place."

Dreyfus began to bleat like a sheep.

"Naturally I have had your office—excuse me, my office—completely redone. It is quite attractive now . . . mauve walls, puce water cooler, lime latrine with apricot toilet paper. A man can get an astonishing amount of work done under pleasant conditions." Clouseau shrugged. "I am beginning to make my mark on Paris. Certain politicians have come forward with the suggestion that I run for public office."

"God help the republic." Dreyfus giggled.

"I beg your pardon?" Clouseau slid down the bench toward Dreyfus to hear.

"I said you can count on my vote," babbled Dreyfus. By now he was rapidly losing control, alternately crossing himself and spitting, and knocking wood.

"Who knows?" Clouseau stood up and adopted a presidential pose. "I might find a place for you in my Cabinet."

The bench tipped up and Dreyfus slid onto the ground. As Clouseau watched in horrified surprise, Dreyfus crawled toward some dandelions and began eating them. Clouseau moved to help him. Dreyfus leaped to his feet and stepped squarely on the rake, which flew up and hit him between the eyes.

Clouseau contemplated his former comrade with compassion. "Of course this is only my opinion, but you appear to be in no condition to serve as Minister of Defense in my Cabinet."

"I'm fine." Dreyfus's giggle rose to a hysterical shriek. "I'm perfect! Every day in every way I'm getting better and better."

Dreyfus's cracked voice, the product of his cracked

mind, rose in song. Out on the lake the swans swam in angry little circles, biting themselves.

"You must get a grip on yourself," Clouseau admonished. "I'm afraid this is not your day. I advise you to postpone your appearance before the wacko board until you are in better shape. Between you and me, old friend," Clouseau confided, "you still are crazy as a bedbug."

Dreyfus glared at Clouseau and drew himself up into a Napoleonic stance.

"It is my day!" he screamed. "After eighteen long, terrible months here among these loonies and weirdos, I will not permit anything to spoil it! *Can you get that through your thick, wretched, cretinous cranium?*"

Clouseau shrugged and looked at the ground.

Dreyfus took Clouseau's face in both hands and squeezed his cheeks until tears flooded Clouseau's eyes. "I am going to walk you to your car." Dreyfus, his fingers dug into Clouseau's cheeks, began to drag him in the direction of the visitor's parking area. "And I am going to kiss you bye-bye. And you are going to drive away in your nice new car—which should rightly be mine—and then the Sanity Commission is going to review my case and set me free! And we are all going to live happily ever after!"

The inmate in the American Indian headdress rose from his place of concealment behind a pink oleander bush and shot a rubber-suction-tipped arrow smack into the middle of Dreyfus's brow. Growls began emerging from Dreyfus's foam-flecked lips. His eyelid twitched ominously as he reached for Clouseau's unprotected throat.

"I have a wonderful idea," Dreyfus prattled. "Let's kill you!"

In the board room of the Administration Building, the three eminent psychiatrists who had driven from, respectively, Rouen, Marseille, and Nancy for the sanity hearing, awaited the appearance of the patient. Dr. Duval took the occasion to brief his colleagues on Dreyfus's miraculous and dramatic recovery. The case, he announced, represented a significant breakthrough in the successful treatment of the most pronounced form of insanity.

The figure of Clouseau appeared briefly outside the windows of the board room. Clouseau gave the appearance of a man running for his life. The psychiatrists exchanged uneasy glances. Then Dreyfus charged across the walkway in pursuit of Clouseau.

"Your patient?" The psychiatrist from Rouen indicated Dreyfus. Duval nodded miserably.

"Some breakthrough," opined the psychiatrist from Nancy.

"You are out of your frigging mind," announced the psychiatrist from Marseille.

Dr. Duval picked up the Dreyfus case records and folders from the desk. "You win some and you lose some." He smiled. "Care to join me in an absinthe?"

3

In fashion-conscious Paris, one of the lesser-known boutiques was the establishment of Monsieur Auguste Balls, Sixty Nine Rue de Cochon. Situated on the Left Bank, up an alley and around the corner from a mattress-recycling plant, the Balls establishment catered to the whims and humors of a very small, very select clientele. Among its older, more loyal customers was the eminent police inspector, Jacques Clouseau.

He stood in the tiny shoppe, allowing his gaze to pass over the familiar display cases with their bizarre merchandise. Balls catered to customers with a penchant for disguise. There were shelves and rows and rack upon rack of false body parts. These ranged from chests and breasts (uptilted, sagging, pear-shaped, melon-shaped, egg-shaped) to stomachs (potbellied, beerbellied) and buttocks (fat asses, bubble butts; cheeky, ultra-cheeky).

The facial corner offered false noses of all shapes and sizes as well as eyes, eyebrows, ears—some with scar tissue—lips, chins, and brows. There was row upon row of wigs plus racks of uniforms, garments, capes, coats, cloaks, boots, shoes, and slippers.

Of particular pride to the proprietor, a tall starveling in his sixties, was the so-called Wound Room. Here a variety of bodily injuries were offered for sale. There were fake razor scars and stab wounds, gunshot wounds, bloodied bandages and dressings, scabs, pustules and sores to suit even the most discriminating taste. The drawers of a small escritoire held a profusion of warts, wens, pimples, and other skin blemishes.

"What can I do for you, Inspector?" Balls greeted his favorite customer.

"As you can see, I have come for my final fitting," said Clouseau nodding. "And if all goes well, perhaps later you can show me something in an abscess."

"Of course." Balls led the way to a small fitting room curtained off from the shop proper by mildewed velvet drapes on which, it was claimed, gargoyles had once vomited. Balls seized a speaking tube and shouted into it.

"Cunny! Inspector Clouseau is here for his final fitting." Balls smiled at his customer. "I think you will be pleased. It turned out better than we dared hope."

Cunny the tailor sidled into the fitting room carrying Clouseau's made-to-measure disguise. Cunny was a small hunchback gypsy of indeterminate age and decided halitosis, which he managed to conceal by the simple expedient of never bathing.

While Balls amused Clouseau by trying on a variety of noses for him, Cunny fitted the customer with a cape under which he had cleverly constructed a custom hump more realistic than his own. Cunny attached a short tube leading from a helium cylinder to the hump.

Balls beamed. "I call this the Hunchback of Notre Dame. Cunny, of course, I call the Hunchback of

Hungary. Also, I call him 'you little bastard,' but only when I am provoked with him."

Balls turned Clouseau so that his image was equally displayed in separate panels of a three-way mirror. Clouseau examined his image critically. He nodded. "Very nice."

"When it comes to designing humps," Ball boasted, "Cunny is without peer."

"Ask the man who owns one, eh?" Clouseau chortled. He gave Cunny a friendly kick in the shin. "Let's blow the damn thing up."

Cunny opened the valve on the cylinder of helium. The hump on Clouseau's back began to inflate. "More," ordered Clouseau to the Hunchback of Hungary. "After all, I am taller, younger, and more important than you. Therefore I should have a bigger hump." Clouseau turned to Balls. "Is this contraption difficult to operate?"

Balls shook his head. "A child could do it. Simply turn this valve and inflate to the desired degree of disfigurement. Now, may I show you something in a carbuncle?"

Clouseau declined brusquely. Balls persisted. "We're running a special on acne."

"Perhaps some other time," Clouseau conceded. "Tonight I am not in the mood for acne."

Balls surveyed Clouseau critically. "If you want my opinion, you could use a neck boil or two. It would go nicely with the hump."

"Just wrap my package and I'll be off. I'm in a bit of a rush," Clouseau explained.

Balls picked up the frayed speaking tube and shouted into it.

"Marta! Wrap the Inspector's package! There's a love."

While they waited, Balls continued his hard sell. "I've done something daring in a stump. Arm and leg. The complete kit only nine hundred francs."

Clouseau declined with the observation that in emergencies stumps tended to get in the way. Balls, not to be dissuaded, adroitly stuck a fake wax chin and brow on Clouseau's face.

"Incredible," commented the proprietor. "It changes your appearance completely."

Marta entered the fitting room and started to wrap the hump-disguise costume. "You remember Inspector Clouseau?" Balls queried.

"I never saw this gentleman before in my life," Marta insisted.

"You see?" observed a gleeful Balls. He removed the wax chin and brow. Clouseau bowed to Marta and offered a courtly good evening. Marta nearly fainted. Her hand flew to her mouth. "Inspector!" she gasped. "I cannot believe my eyes!"

"That is because your husband is a genius." Clouseau smiled. "Please wrap them up." He handed Marta the wax chin and brow. "And," he pointed at Marta's nose, "throw in the nose."

Marta giggled. "It is impossible," Balls thundered.

Clouseau was adamant. "Money is no object. I must have that nose. It is positively the ugliest nose I have ever seen."

"It is also Marta's own nose," Balls retorted in a fit of pique.

"My compliments, madame," cooed Clouseau. "It suits you."

4

Upon his promotion from simple police inspector to Chief Inspector, Jacques Clouseau drastically effected a change in his style of living. That is to say he moved from his ratty little pied-à-terre cold-water flat in the market district to a larger, ratty, and outrageously overpriced apartment in a far better section of Paris overlooking the municipal gasworks.

Even as the unsuspecting Clouseau was en route home, a Sinister Figure in black prowled the apartment directly below Clouseau's. Charles Dreyfus, madman and recent asylum escapee, was bent on revenge. Otherwise, one might ask, why was Dreyfus equipped with explosives, fuses, detonators, and wiring in sufficient quantity to blow the entire sixteenth arrondissement into the Seine?

Whistling with the happy unconcern of a man in utter contentment at the end of an honest day's work, Clouseau sauntered up the sidewalk and unlocked the front door of the building. Humming to himself, Clouseau stepped into the lift and, for once, pressed the correct button for the fourth floor.

Meanwhile, in the darkened apartment directly below on the third floor, Dreyfus selected a long, wicked-looking drill from his bag of tricks and set to work drilling a hole in the ceiling of the vestibule.

The elevator arrived at the fourth floor. Clouseau got off. A pretty young woman, possibly an Avon saleslady, sauntered down the corridor to the elevator. Clouseau, ever the appreciator of fine art, inserted his key in the door without removing the key ring from the long chain he carried. The pretty young woman dropped a parcel. Clouseau swooped forward to collect it and tore out the front panel of his trousers as the stout key chain refused to give way. The pretty young woman giggled, Clouseau blushed, the elevator arrived, and love died aborning.

Had Clouseau's mind been on other things than legs, he might have noticed the small periscope being pushed up through the floor of his vestibule from below. Instead, he hung up his coat, saw it slide off the coat hanger to the floor, shrugged, and entered the living room calling for Cato, his faithful and long-suffering Japanese houseboy.

There was no response. Clouseau tensed, every nerve and muscle alert. He moved forward, into the bathroom. Behind him, through the floor, Dreyfus drilled another hole through which to insert his mini-periscope. This time, success! By twisting his head to

15

an agonizing angle, Dreyfus was able to see Clouseau through his periscope, much as a U-boat captain in wartime must have sighted in on an unsuspecting cargo ship. Dreyfus tracked Clouseau into the kitchen area overhead, then moved into the third-floor apartment kitchen and drilled a nice, neat hole in the ceiling.

What Clouseau was doing was playing a game. A long-established game in which he and Cato delighted. The game was called hide-and-kill and its rules were simplicity itself. They called for Cato to hide and attack his master from the most devilishly designed ambuscades. Usually, as a reward for his ingenuity, Clouseau beat the shit out of the faithful Cato, who nevertheless managed to get in a few lethal karate blows of his own before being rendered senseless by one of Clouseau's deliberate fouls. Both hunter and hunted took great pains in these periodic tests of skill, although invariably Cato's pains were the more severe.

Clouseau tiptoed about the kitchen, sniffing, listening, remembering past Cato plays. There was the time in '75 when Cato had taken him quite unawares by launching a murderous attack from inside the freezer. Clouseau tensed and yanked open the refrigerator door. A bottle of ketchup and several onions rolled off the shelf in the refrigerator and smashed on the floor. As Clouseau moved cautiously into the laundry area, Dreyfus's drill popped up through the already spreading puddle of ketchup on the kitchen floor.

Dreyfus put his eye to the drill hole in the ceiling. Ketchup dripped into his face. A premature shout of elation at the sight of Clouseau's blood being spilled died in Dreyfus's throat.

Clouseau's eyes darted to a basket of fresh laundry. Might not the wily Cato be hiding under the sheets? Only one way to find out. Clouseau opened his mouth in the terrible karate cry of attack and leaped into the basket. Shirts, socks, pillowcases, underwear, and pajamas went flying. The action dislodged the ironing board from its fold-up position in the wall directly behind Clouseau. The board fell out and into the upright position. Clouseau whirled and delivered a vicious chop, splitting the board in half and dropping the heavy steam iron on his instep. Clouseau yelped in pain.

Under the laundry sink Dreyfus's drill bit into a hot-water pipe. Steaming water poured into the hole left by the drill. In the apartment below, Dreyfus screamed in agony and frustration.

Clouseau turned his apartment upside down, seeking the elusive Cato and not finding him. Yet the Little Yellow Skin, as Clouseau affectionately called Cato, had to be hidden somewhere. Only the bedroom was left. Clouseau searched the room carefully, checked in closets, looked under the canopied bed, even climbed onto a chair and looked on top of the canopy. There was not a trace of Cato. Baffled, Clouseau slumped onto the bed and stretched out on his back.

Clouseau closed his eyes, then they clicked open in horror. There, spread-eagled in the frame on the underside of the canopy, crouched the deadly Cato. With a fiendish cry he dropped onto Clouseau.

Oh, the joy of combat! For fully twenty minutes they fought, wrestled, punched, kicked, gouged, kneed, bit, spat, clawed in the very best of spirits. Drapes were torn, tables overturned, mirrors smashed. Cato, nearly done in, paused, gasping for breath on a throw rug. Clouseau grabbed the near end of the rug and gave a mighty yank, thinking to jerk Cato off his feet. Cato anticipated his master's move and jumped high in the air. Clouseau only succeeded in entangling himself in the rug. Cato good-naturedly kicked Clouseau in the kidney. Mercifully, the telephone rang. Cato went to the kitchen and picked up the instrument.

"Chief Inspector Clouseau's residence," he gasped. "One moment, sir."

Cato held out the phone to Clouseau. "For you. The Deputy Commissioner."

Angered at having been outwitted, Clouseau

snatched the phone away from Cato and gave himself a terrible blow on the jaw. In a daze he heard the Deputy Commissioner warn him that Dreyfus had escaped from the insane asylum and might be headed for Paris to kill his fancied tormentor, Clouseau.

In the apartment below, Dreyfus set about planting his explosive charges.

"I understand, sir," Clouseau neared the end of his telephone conversation. "Thank you for calling . . . Yes, I shall take every precaution." He held out the phone to Cato. "Hang up for me."

As Cato obediently took the phone and turned to hang it up, Clouseau viciously chopped him across the neck with his free hand. Cato dropped in his tracks.

"Very careless of you," Clouseau chided. "You forgot the first rule of self-defense: Never do your adversary a favor unless he is unconscious. Now, stop lying there and get out my disguise kit! The time for work has come."

Although hemorrhaging internally, Cato pulled himself to the bedroom closet and took down the box from Balls with the large label: "Helium Hunchback Kit." Below that, in red letters, appeared the following legend: "Warning—do not overinflate." Impatiently, Clouseau tore the wrapping from the package and, with Cato's assistance, began to put on his hunchback disguise. Annoyingly, the telephone rang. This time Clouseau snatched it up. "Hello."

In the apartment below, Dreyfus stifled an anticipatory giggle as he carried on his end of the telephone conversation with the unsuspecting Clouseau. Dreyfus passed himself off as a member of a citizen's appreciation committee anxious to honor Inspector Clouseau for his years of meritorious service to the department and to the community. As Clouseau listened, enchanted, Cato connected the helium tank to the inflatable hump on Clouseau's back. Then he opened the valve.

The hump began to inflate.

Bigger and bigger grew the bag. Clouseau was so

busy being modest and murmuring things like "You are very kind," "Just dong my job," and the ever-popular "All in a day's work" that he failed to notice his feet no longer were touching the floor. Clouseau began to sway gently to and fro in the air, his toes six inches off the carpet.

Down below, Dreyfus skillfully manipulated the telephone and the detonators leading to a huge wad of plastique affixed to the ceiling.

"You wish to bestow a medal on me?" Clouseau could scarcely believe his ears. "Yes, of course. I shall be delighted to accept. The pleasure is all mine." A gentle breeze wafted Clouseau into his bedroom and out the French windows into the balmy, Parisian night. Clouseau never relaxed his grip on the telephone. "Yes, I have replaced the lunatic Dreyfus as Chief Inspector," he admitted.

"I am sure Paris sleeps the more safely because of the change," cooed Dreyfus, ably disguising his voice. "And that killers, thieves and assassins tremble in their shoes."

Clouseau was on the point of murmuring something to the effect of "You are too kind" when he became aware of Cato's frantic face gazing at him from the window. But Cato was inside the window looking *out*. Clouseau thought about that. Clouseau looked *down* upon the city. Seeing he was airborne, Clouseau gasped and dropped the phone.

The telephone swung in a lovely, wide arc through the open window of the third-floor apartment and struck the fiend Dreyfus on the back of the skull, knocking him flat on his face across the detonator. There was a tremendous explosion. The building's upper floor vanished in a cloud of paster dust and rubble. The shock wave sent Clouseau and his plastic hump soaring over Paris like some great fat bird.

On the streets below, tourists looked skyward and their mouths fell open. Two nuns emerging from Notre Dame Cathedral, crossed themselves and fell to their knees. On the river, a sightseeing boat rammed the far bank and ran aground. A cyclist watching Clouseau float overhead lost his way and rode off the Bir-Hakeim bridge into the Seine. Like a human Zeppelin, Clouseau wafted on his way above the great city.

Clouseau found flying in this fashion an exhilarating experience. He wondered if he might patent this great invention. He heard a small hiss of escaping helium. Suddenly, Clouseau began to wonder about such things as where he might fall and how many of his bones might be expected to break.

5

At the Sûreté, François poured hot coffee and carried it into Clouseau's office. The Deputy Commissioner paced in agitation as he studied the still-sodden and shaking Clouseau, who nonetheless sat bravely at his desk, making gallant little puddles on the floor.

"Have you received a report from the bomb squad?" The Deputy Commissioner sat down and reached for a cigarette. Clouseau opened a desk drawer, found a lighter, and lighted the cigarette.

"No. However, my instinct tells me it was most definitely a beum," Clouseau speculated.

"A beum?" The Deputy Commissioner appeared puzzled.

"What?" shot back Clouseau.

"You said a 'beum,'" explained the Deputy Commissioner gently. He realized Clouseau had been through a lot. "What sort of bomb is a beum?"

"The exploding kind," Clouseau snarled. Deputy Commissioners were such fools. Didn't the man realize what he had been through this night? "Actually, I am fortunate to be alive. Poor Cato, my trusted

Oriental houseboy, is in the hospital. He looks like a charred banana."

The Deputy Commissioner reached for the coffee-pot as Clouseau stood up to shake his hand. "I was about to say good night," Clouseau announced, "but I see you have spilled coffee all over your white shirt front. Never fear, a little cold soda water and the shirt is good as new."

Clouseau seized a Seltzer bottle from the portable bar behind his desk and doused the Deputy Commissioner.

"Why don't you go f—" sputtered the Deputy Commissioner as a jet of soda water squirted him in the face.

"I beg your pardon," said Clouseau. "What was it that you were saying?"

"I was saying why don't you go find a place to recuperate." The Deputy Commissioner had managed to regain control. "You should take a long rest. I'll see someone else is assigned to the case."

"Absolutely not!" Clouseau was angry. "This was a deliberate attempt on my life. And no one but I shall bring the mad beumer to justice!"

The Deputy Commissioner stood up to take his leave. "I admire your spunk, Clouseau."

"Never mind my spunk," that worthy shot back. "Just change that shirt when you get home. And the sooner the better."

Later, after the Deputy Commissioner had left and three janitors had finished mopping up the water around Clouseau's desk, François stuck his head in the door and almost caught Clouseau playing with a Yo-Yo. Clouseau barely had time to drop the toy into his desk drawer.

"Excellent for manual dexterity." He grimaced. "What is it, François?"

"Before you go home, could you sign this?" François laid some papers on the desktop. Clouseau affixed his signature without bothering to read the document.

"It's the order transferring Tournier, the bank robber, to prison," François said.

"Society is well rid of that one," Clouseau muttered. "By God, he was a slippery swine to catch, eh?"

But François and the signed document were gone.

A few miles from the site of the original Bastille stands a modern prison. Parisians call it the New Bastille. But to the underworld it is known as the Dungeon of the Damned. Escape from this maximum-security institution is impossible.

While Clouseau sat in his office playing with his Yo-Yo, a taxicab halted outside the impenetrable walls of the New Bastille. Out of the taxi's rear window, poor old crazy Charles Dreyfus aimed a bazooka at the prison and calmly blew a six-foot hole in the building. Prison Inmate 66584229, also known as Tournier the Bank Robber, walked out through the flying debris and climbed into the taxi beside the gleeful Dreyfus. Even as the first police sirens began to be heard, the taxi drove off and vanished among the back alleys of Paris.

6

Paris Match gave the daring prison escape story three columns and a picture. The *Herald Tribune* put it on page one, above the Panama Canal crisis. The *Christian Science Monitor* gave Tournier a box alongside the Help Wanted ads. In every leading newspaper throughout the world, the exploit was big news.

Clouseau sat in his office, reading the day's papers and fuming. He stuffed the bowl of his pipe, struck a large wooden match, lit the pipe and, without bothering to take the pipe from his mouth, blew out the match. In the process he managed to spray glowing coals from the pipe bowl across the newspapers covering his desk.

22

Paris Match began to smolder. The *Herald Tribune* burst into flame. Clouseau picked up the paper and looked about for a place to dump it. His wastebasket was full. Coals on the front page of the *Herald Tribune* quickly burned through to the back page and wound up on the desktop like so many particles of burning lava. Clouseau inhaled a mighty gulp of air and blew the burning coals off his desktop onto the rug, where they began to smolder anew.

Clouseau did an Indian fire dance on the rug while holding onto the burning newspaper. The paper got too hot to hold. Clouseau got rid of it in the wastebasket, which now began to burn like a prairie fire. In desperation he snatched up the water carafe on his desk and dumped it upside down over the flames. Zounds! The carafe was empty!

Clouseau pulled off his jacket and threw it over the wastebasket, hoping to smother the flames. For the moment he succeeded. Thick white smoke billowed from the wastebasket and started to fill the room. Clouseau ran to the window and pulled at it. The window was stuck. Clouseau climbed onto a chair and tried to lower the upper half of the window. He lost his balance, teetered, swayed, and in desperation grabbed onto the drapes. Clouseau fell, pulling down drapes and window shade with him.

By now the wastebasket was a veritable Vesuvius of flame and choking smoke. Clouseau snatched it off the floor to carry it outside. At the door he fumbled with the knob, shifting the basket and its burning contents to his other arm. Flames from the fire in the basket licked at the sprinkler system. Man-made rain began to fall in Clouseau's office.

Eventually the fires went out. Clouseau put his still-smoldering jacket back on. The jacket was minus most of the right sleeve as well as the breast pocket. A sizable hole had been burned in the rear, just below the pinch back.

Clouseau inspected his likeness in the mirror. He looked like a French smudgepot. What was it Dreyfus had said? Something about a man's ability to command the respect of those under him by his appearance? Yes, that was it. Clouseau left the building by the freight elevator.

Marc of Morocco was a gentlemen's clothier about as far off the beaten track as it is possible to get without leaving town. "Insta-Suit" proclaimed a large sign in the front window. "Clothes Made to Measure While You Wait."

Clouseau, resplendent in a hideous yellow-and-orange plaid suit, stepped jauntily from the interior of Marc of Morocco just as a junk wagon came around the corner. The junk wagon was pulled by an ancient swaybacked horse whose tattered blanket was the exact pattern as the new garments worn proudly by Chief Inspector Clouseau, the nattiest dresser on the force.

While Clouseau was being measured and outfitted in his new finery, a unique robbery was taking place across Paris in the Banque Crédit de Monaco. The guard on duty paid scarce attention to the three maintenance men in jumpers who moved ever so politely among the bank's customers.

If the guard had looked closely at the line of customers before window 3, he might have recognized Tournier the Bank Robber and Escapee. But the guard's attention was on Madeleine LeBeau, the teller at window 3, or, to be more specific, on the sweater Madeleine LeBeau was wearing. The sweater was several sizes too small for Madeleine and the guard was beginning to perspire heavily.

Mopping his brow and fantasizing what he would like to do with, to, and on the aforementioned Mademoiselle LeBeau in the supply closet, should the opportunity arise, the guard never noticed Tournier and two associates step from the line of customers to range themselves alongside the three pretend maintenance men. Machine guns appeared from under jumpers and coveralls. Cash drawers were inverted over canvas sacks. And the guard dreamed his erotic little dreams.

Clouseau confronted the Deputy Commissioner.

"How much did they get?" They were in Clouseau's office with François.

"Three million," François responded. "It is in the report."

The Deputy Commissioner extracted a cigar from his case. Clouseau snatched the lighter from his desk drawer and whipped a flame under the nose of the Deputy Commissioner. Clouseau was in the act of returning the lighter to the drawer when an item in the report caught his eye. Without realizing what he was doing, Clouseau dropped the still-burning lighter in the drawer and pushed it closed.

"Do you think," the Deputy Commissioner speculated, squinting down the length of his cigar, "that there is a connection between the Tournier escape and the bank robbery?"

"You mean because Tournier has been identified as one of the bank robbers?" Clouseau parried, skillfully fighting for time.

"Yes." the Deputy Commissioner blew a perfect smoke ring. "That is precisely why. What do you think?"

Clouseau leaped to his feet. "I think my desk is on fire, that is what I think! François! Call the fire department, if you please!"

The seemingly unrelated wave of crime sweeping the world continued. That evening, in a comfortable, snug English village in Hartfordshire, two masked men broke into the country home of a man named Fassbender and literally kidnapped the good professor out of his bathtub. Also snatched in the kidnap operation was Fassbender's attractive daughter, Margo.

As the Fassbenders were being carried unconscious from the sprawling estate, Jarvis the butler was roused by the careless slamming of a door and got up from his bed to investigate. Doors that slam at 3:00 A.M. are a rarity in Hartfordshire.

For his troubles, Jarvis was shot with a tranquilizing gun by one of the two kidnappers, but not before he managed to get a glimpse of the pair of scoundrels. A powerful man, albeit a devout homosexual, Jarvis was able to crawl halfway across the lawn before collapsing into unconsciousness.

In Scotland Yard, lights burned through the night in the Senior Officers' Lavatory, where a great deal of planning in the unending war against crime went on.

Hugh McLaren, Director of Section 11, had not closed his eyes all night and looked it. When he walked into the loo, intending to splash cold water on his face, he found his colleague Alec Drummond yawning and endeavoring to shave with an electric razor.

"You look a bit grotty," Drummond offered by way of greeting. "Been here all night?" McLaren nodded. "Me too."

Drummond loosened his belt and farted. "The old forces of evil are working overtime, laddie. Bank hold-ups the past twelve hours in Liverpool, Chicago, Milan, and Johannesburg. Plus a whopping train robbery outside Stuttgart. Maybe I'm getting a bit senile, but I can't help feeling there's a connection somewhere."

"My section, too," belched McLaren. "Within the past five days, four of the world's most dangerous killers have broken jail."

"Do tell." Drummond tried to get rid of a tiny gas bubble and succeeded in staining his shorts. McLaren never noticed.

"That Mafia chap—Something the Knife—escaped from Leavenworth. On the same day Cairo Fred went over the wall at Khartoum. Then, less then twenty-four hours later, Hindu Harry the Sniper got clean away from a maximum-security facility in India. To top it all, last night the Hong Kong Strangler broke out of death row at the California Women's Prison at Tehachapi literally hours before she was to be executed."

McLaren and Drummond looked up as Superintendent Quinlan entered, nodded, and sat down in the farthest cubicle.

"Heard the latest?" Quinlan invited, dropping his trousers. "Somebody kidnapped Hugo Fassbender and his daughter."

A low whistle escaped McLaren, a man not readily shaken. *"The* Hugo Fassbender?"

"The same," grunted Quinlan. "Paris has a theory. Don't ask me why—they're sending their top man to help us. Chief Inspector Clouseau." Quinlan cheerily waved a telegram. "He just sent this wire. 'Arrive Heathrow, B.A. flight 3, 12:38 P.M. I shall be in disguise. Clouseau.' Be good chaps and go fetch him, will you? I may be here all day," groaned Quinlan who suffered from constipation.

"What kind of disguise?" Drummond queried. In the Yard, it was conceded that Drummond has a mind like a steel trap.

"He doesn't say," replied Quinlan with a wince.

"Then how the devil are we going to recognize him?" asked McLaren, a studious sort and rather slow-witted, but considered to be something of a comer.

"That," rasped Quinlan, "would appear to be your problem."

7

British Airways Flight 3, nonstop Paris to London, sliced through contrails thirty thousand feet above the English Channel. Two stewardesses jockeyed a cocktail tray down the aisle of the first class compartment. The head-bandaged gentleman with the leg cast in seat A-4 kept his exposed eye on the illuminated sign over the door to the restroom. Chief Inspector Clouseau had things other than cocktails on his mind. The sign continued to read "occupied." Clouseau sighed and shifted his leg to a more comfortable position, allowing the cast to project several inches into the aisle.

The lead stewardess, a veteran with British Airways, deftly avoided the big toe protruding in her direction and continued on her way, spreading joy and Irish whiskey. Over the loo the sign winked to "Vacant."

Clouseau got to his feet and limped down the aisle. He entered the loo and shut the door. In the tiny cubicle Clouseau rested his crutches against the wall and sat down. That is, he tried to sit down. The cast on his leg effectively prevented that. Because of the length of the rigid cast, which stretched from instep to thigh, there was no way for Clouseau to sit down.

Clouseau thought hard, searching for a solution. Finally, he opened the loo door and let his straight, cast-encased leg stick out into the passenger compartment. A woman teacher with fourteen sixth-grade children averted her eyes. The sixth-graders thoughtfully autographed Clouseau's cast. Flight 3 droned on its way as though nothing untoward had occurred.

With some struggling, Clouseau managed to lift his cast-weighted leg straight up over his head, which permitted him to get the door almost shut. In the pilot's compartment, Senior Pilot John Andrews turned over the controls to his copilot and sauntered down the aisle to the loo. He opened the door and promptly was knocked senseless when the heavy cast on Clouseau's leg hit him on the head.

At Heathrow Airport, Alec Drummond looked curiously at the St. George's Hospital ambulance streaking out to meet arriving British Airways Flight 3. The jaunty Trident touched down and taxied to a stop. Passengers began to disembark. McLaren consulted the photograph of Chief Inspector Clouseau in his hand. None of the passengers even remotely resembled the famous French detective.

An airline attendant pushed a wheelchair to the foot of the steps of the Trident and looked up at Clouseau, who was maneuvering his crutches in the doorway of the plane. "May I help, sir?"

Clouseau waved the man aside. "I am perfectly

able to take care of myself." Clouseau placed his crutches on the edge of the first step, shifted his weight to his good leg, lost his balance, and fell down the stairs, in the process taking a fat lady and her pet griffon with him. The fat lady landed atop her dog, which upset her no end.

Clouseau instantly assumed control of the situation. "Put her in my wheelchair." He made the woman as comfortable as possible, not realizing that his head bandage had started to unwind and that the fat lady was sitting on the loose end.

"Get this poor unfortunate woman to a hospital immediately," Clouseau ordered. An attendant trotted off, pushing the wheelchair. Clouseau's bandage began to unwind, spinning him like a top. Drummond tapped him on the shoulder, no mean feat considering the dizzying speed with which Clouseau was rotating. "Inspector Clouseau?"

Clouseau eyed the two suspicious characters and tried to make the horizon stop whirling. If ever he spotted two classic criminal types! The smaller of the two was holding out his hand.

"I'm Drummond from Scotland Yard." Clouseau alertly played his part in the simple ruse.

"And I am André Butot, mustard salesman from Dijon," Clouseau lied glibly. To his credit, Drummond never lost his composure.

"May I offer you a lift into London, Monsieur Butot?"

Clouseau bowed. "That would be most kind of you, Mr. Yard."

"Drummond," corrected Drummond. McLaren crammed both his fists into his mouth to keep himself from laughing.

"If you insist," said Clouseau mincingly. And he followed McLaren and Drummond to where an official car from Scotland Yard waited at the edge of the tarmak. Between them, Drummond and McLaren managed to get Clouseau and his leg case into the rear seat of their Panda car. As the car headed for

London, Clouseau's cast came sailing out the window and smashed to pieces on the windscreen of a taxi bearing the Ambassador of Uganda to the departure area.

8

At the Fassbender estate, police constables and detectives were conducting a thorough search of the grounds despite a chilling rain that was systematically washing away any semblance of clues. Livestock, huddled in the capacious but snug barns, watched the human idiots running around outside in the downpour and then returned to their cuds.

A police car pulled up in the driveway and stopped among the other police vehicles, which had been on the scene since the sensational kidnapping. The driver got out, opening an umbrella, and stepped to the rear door just as his passenger, Clouseau, opened the rear door on the opposite side and got out. Clouseau held up his hand and peered intently into the sodden skies. "The barometer is falling," he muttered to no one in particular. "Make a note of that."

The driver, hearing Clouseau talking to himself, thrust the umbrella into the Inspector's hand and withdrew to a safe distance.

Starting toward the Fassbender farmhouse, Clouseau stepped into the middle of a large puddle. When he withdrew his foot, it was shoeless. Clouseau's big toe thrust coquettishly through the ragged hole in his sock. "Darn," he observed. "In fact, *merde*."

Acting out of habit, Clouseau's driver, a former gentleman's gentleman, rolled up his sleeve and felt around in the muck until he was able to retrieve Clouseau's shoe. He held it up triumphantly. Rivulets of water ran through the two holes that had been worn in the sole. Clouseau snatched the shoe and after several fruitless attempts to put it on while standing storklike on one leg, hopped across the yard to the front door, shoe in hand.

Clouseau leaned up against the front gate for support. Once again he tried to slip his foot into the mucky shoe, lost his balance, and fell full length into a bed of peonies and bluebells. The shoe flew from Clouseau's hand, landing several yards to one side, where a young and extremely earnest young constable named Robbins was searching for clues on his hands and knees.

"Halloo!" Robbins called out. "I've found something."

"What is it?" asked a senior detective.

"Looks like a shoe." Robbins held up his find.

"It most assuredly is a shoe." Clouseau limped over to Robbins. "I am Chief Inspector Clouseau and that is my shoe."

The senior detective looked at Robbins. "No offense, Inspector, but how do we know it's your shoe?"

"Because," said Clouseau, choosing his words carefully in the manner of one dealing with mental inferiors, "it should be obvious even to you that I am wearing only one shoe."

"Right you are, sir."

"It should also be obvious that the shoe I am wearing is the mate to that shoe."

The senior detective shook his head. Clouseau looked at Constable Robbins, who also shook his head. "They're not even the same color, sir."

Clouseau glanced down at the black shoe on his left foot and at the brown shoe the detective was examining. Section Director Drummond came out of the house and made his way to Clouseau.

"What's going on?"

The senior detective winked at Drummond. "This gentleman claims to be the famous Chief Inspector Clouseau from France. He says this is his shoe."

31

Drummond turned to Clouseau. "Is it?" Clouseau nodded. "Give it to him."

Drummond took Clouseau's arm and began steering him toward the front door. "Doubtless you are going to tell me you have another pair exactly like this one at home," Drummond deadpanned.

Clouseau's eyes widened in astonishment. "How did you know?"

At the front door, Clouseau and Drummond reached simultaneously for the heavy brass door knocker. Clouseau managed to slam it on Drummond's fingers. "There is British craftsmanship for you," Clouseau sneered. "Give me an old-fashioned bell-pull anytime."

He whirled as the front door was opened from the inside by Jarvis the butler. "Quickly, my man! What is your name? And no tricks!"

"Jarvis, sir." The butler took Clouseau's hat and coat and shoe to hang them up. Clouseau snatched back the shoe.

"A likely story." Clouseau indicated to Drummond that he intended to pursue cross-examining this key witness. Drummond rolled his eyes and went off toward the kitchen in search of crumpets. "And what is it that you do, Jarvis?" Clouseau kept his eyes riveted on the man.

"I am the butler."

"Now we are getting somewhere."

Clouseau began walking in a circle around Jarvis. "And were you the butler last night, during the kidnapping?" Jarvis, turning his head to follow Clouseau, practically dislocated his neck by nodding. "And would you mind telling me where you were on the night of August fourth between the hours of ten and seven o'clock P.M.?" Clouseau thundered.

"Asleep in my room," Jarvis said evasively.

"Asleep in your reum," Clouseau mimicked. "I suppose you can prove it?" Jarvis shook his head. "I see," Clouseau noted. Already the case was beginning to fall into neat little components. Clouseau put on his shoe and instructed a detective who was flipping through a back issue of *Punch* to have the household staff assemble in the living room immediately. Jarvis began to move away. Clouseau was too quick for him and grasped the butler by the collar.

"Where do you think you are going?" hissed Clouseau.

"To the living room, sir. To be questioned with the rest of the staff. You just gave the order yourself."

"I am glad to see you are paying attention." Clouseau suddenly switched to his charm technique, which he had found to be an invaluable ploy in throwing suspects off their guard. "Now, why don't you show me about this charming little hut? Beginning with the upstairs?"

Jarvis led the way. Clouseau searched carefully and made frequent, if illegible notes in the peculiar scawl that he had managed to develop over the years. "It is my own style of shorthand," he explained when he caught Jarvis trying to read over his shoulder in Margo Fassbender's room. "And I defy anyone to read it. The code is so foolproof," he confided, "there are times when I am unable to read it myself."

Apart from several albums, an autographed photograph of a movie star stuck in her dressing-table mirror, and a bank statement that showed she was recklessly overdrawn, Margo's room surrendered little of interest. In Professor Fassbender's room across the hall, Clouseau irritably pawed through notebooks crammed with formulas and computations.

"Drivel." Clouseau dumped the accumulation of a life's work in the wastebasket. "Absolute gibberish. I cannot imagine why anyone would wish to kidnap such an obvious idiot, particularly an idiot with a daughter unable to keep her own bank account in order. We might as well go downstairs. We are obviously wasting out time up here."

Jarvis led Clouseau down the hall. At the door to the bathroom he halted.

"No thank you," Clouseau shook his head. "I do not have to make peepee just yet."

Jarvis's features remained immobile. "I assumed you might wish to look for fingerprints."

Clouseau smiled his craftiest smile. "Looking for fingerprints would be the natural thing to do. However, I am a very unnatural detective who owes his extraordinary success to a rare combination of the bizarre, the intuitive, and regular bowel movements."

Clouseau started briskly down the long corridor. He was headed toward the backstairs area when instinct made him stop midway, opposite what appeared to be an ordinary plaster wall. Close examination revealed a small door set flush in the molding. Clouseau rapped with his knuckles and got a decidedly hollow sound. "Why did you not tell me there was a secret door here?" Clouseau asked accusingly.

"You neglected to ask me," Jarvis offered. "In any event, it's not locked."

"Obviously." Clouseau turned the knob. The door opened. Finger to his lips, Clouseau stepped over the threshold into total darkness. Clouseau groped his way forward several paces. "Hello? Anyone home?" There was no answer. He fumbled in his pockets for a match, breaking three before he managed to light one. By its feeble light Clouseau saw what appeared to be an electric switch. He gave it a cautious flip. The match went out. Somewhere in the darkness machinery began to hum.

Clouseau moved forward and lit another match. He kept walking. When this match burned out, he lit another and tried to peer ahead beyond the tiny circle of light, looking for all the world like a rumpled Statue of Liberty.

"Sir?" Clouseau jumped at sound of Jarvis's voice close by. Obviously the man must have followed him deep into some sort of secret passageway. "No tricks," Clouseau warned. "I tried the switch, but the lights do not appear to be working."

"Perhaps you tried the wrong switch, sir." This time Jarvis seemed to be speaking from somewhere up ahead. There was a click and blinding light flooded the small private gymnasium in which they stood. Only then did Clouseau discover he had been walking for what seemed like ages on an electric treadmill.

"Nothing like a brisk walk for the digestion," Clouseau commented as he stepped off the treadmill. He moved curiously among the athletic paraphernalia. There were rings, trapezes, horizontal bars, barbells, incline boards, reducing machines, and even a climbing rope. "Unless I miss my guess," hazarded Clouseau, "this is the gymnasium."

Jarvis watched Clouseau walk between the parallel bars. "In my days at the police academy, I was quite an athlete."

Clouseau grasped the bars and swung up into the press position. Jarvis applauded. Clouseau swung once, twice, vaulted over the bar in a graceful dismount, and disappeared from sight down a staircase he had failed to take note of beside the parallel bars. Clouseau tumbled the length of the stairs and through a door at the foot, finally coming to rest in an upside-down position in the living room in front of Drummond and the entire household staff.

9

Mrs. Japonica, the maid, looked startled at Clouseau's entrance. The housekeeper, Mrs. Leverlilly, made a slight curtsy. The cook, Mr. Bullock, winked at Mr. Stutterstutt, the beekeeper, who had just come in from the hives and still wore his protective head covering. Mr. Shork, the Welsh gardener, stared at his feet.

"Well!" Clouseau got briskly to his feet. "That felt good!" Jarvis entered behind Clouseau and quietly shut the door, glancing disapprovingly at Mr. Shork's mud-smeared boots. Jarvis hated the Welsh. Mr. Shork, who had an instinctive dislike of fags, surreptitiously wiped a generous amount of mud onto the rug.

"I suppose," Clouseau quipped, "you're all wondering why I asked you here."

Clouseau turned to commence what he called his "interrogation stalk" and stepped hard on Mrs. Japonica's foot. The lady howled in pain. Despite her diminutive appearance, Mrs. Japonica had the lungs of an opera star. Clouseau leaped up and collided with a suit of armor. Instinctively, Clouseau fell into his karate pose and chopped at the suit of armor, bringing it crashing to the floor. Helmet, breastplate, shin guards, sword, and flail scattered to the corners of the room. Clouseau graciously moved to help Jarvis collect the pieces of what had been a very fine thirteenth-century knight.

To his annoyance, Clouseau discovered his hand had become firmly jammed into the metal gauntlet holding the flail. The harder he tried to free his hand, the more firmly it remained stuck. To cover his embarrassment, Clouseau clasped his hands behind his back and walked about, feigning unconcern. The only trouble was that every time he took a step the heavy flail swung between his legs and painfully nudged his scrotum. Clouseau abruptly quit moving. This brought him face to face with Shork.

"Your name," Clouseau thundered.

"Shork, the gardener," the wiry Welshman whined.

Clouseau pressed his advantage. "And what is it that you do?"

"I'm the gardener," poor Shork stammered.

"Why didn't you say so in the first place?" Clouseau probed skillfully.

"I did." Shork was close to tears.

"Do not be funny with me, monsieur," Clouseau snarled. "This is a serious matter and everyone in this reum is under suspicion. There is a very good chance that *someone* in his *reum* knows more about the murder than he is telling."

"Murder!" gasped Mrs. Japonica.

"What?" Clouseau whirled, banging himself in the

balls with the flail. "What was that you said?" His voice trailed upward like a lyric soprano's.

"I said murder," bleated Mrs. Japonica.

"What murder?" Clouseau was getting confused. That is, the great detective was deftly creating the illusion of being confused.

"I don't know, but you said murder." Mrs. Japonica suddenly began getting a severe headache.

"*I* said murder?" Clouseau riposted. "*You* said murder!"

"Yes, *I* said murder because *you* said murder." Mrs. Japonica wanted nothing so much as a place to lie down.

"*I* said murder?" said Clouseau incredulously.

It was Shork who saved Mrs. Japonica's sanity. "You said, 'Someone in this room knows more about the murder than he is telling,' " Shork reminded.

"Thank you." Clouseau dropped his voice conspiratorially. "Listen, er, ah, what's your name?"

"Shork," replied Shork. He spelled it out carefully. "S—H—O—R—K."

"The cook," Clouseau remembered.

"The gardener." Shork longed for a drink.

"Now we're getting somewhere." Clouseau smiled.

Clouseau suddenly whipped up his gauntleted hand and pointed directly at Stutterstutt. "You!"

The iron flail swung up and caught Stutterstutt under the chin, knocking him over a chair. Shork helped the dazed beekeeper to his feet. "Are you all right?"

"I demand to know the name of this man!" cried Clouseau. Bullock the cook covered his face with his chef's hat. "He's Mr. Stutterstutt."

"And just what is your job, Mr. Stuckerstuff?" asked Clouseau.

"He told you," said Shork. "Can't you remember anything? He's the beekeeper."

"I want him to tell me that!" Clouseau shouted at Shork, meanwhile pointing at Stutterstutt with his left hand.

"He can't," Shork shrilled triumphantly. "He's caught cold and lost his voice, he has."

Clouseau paused to ponder. A bee began buzzing about his head. "What do we have so far?" Clouseau posed the rhetorical question. "A beekeeper who has lost his voice. A cook who says that he is the gardener. And a witness to a murder, when we assumed we were dealing with a simple double kidnapping. It is obvious that there is more here than meets the eye."

The bee flew away from Clouseau and landed on the piano. Clouseau swung the flail like a fly swatter and tore a gaping hole in the lid of the magnificent Steinway baby grand. Clouseau turned his attention to Stutterstutt.

"I suggest you count your bees. One of them may be missing."

Mrs. Leverlilly went white with shock. "You've ruined the piano," she wailed.

Clouseau remained unruffled. "One piano is of little consequence compared with the terrible crime that has been committed here."

"But that is a priceless Steinway," sobbed Mrs. Leverlilly.

"Not any more," Clouseau admonished. "What is your name, madame?"

"Mrs. Leverlilly," she sniffled into her handkerchief.

Clouseau hazarded a wild guess. "The housekeeper." Mrs. Leverlilly nodded. "That would account for your exaggerated hysteria over a simple blemish on the furniture," concluded Clouseau, who now stood leaning on the ornate mantel of the Jacobean walk-in fireplace. The iron ball at the end of the flail hung barely inches above the dancing flames. The iron ball began to glow. As Clouseau continued speaking the heat began to travel up the length of chain to the handle of the flail itself and thence through the fingers of the metal gauntlet.

"Whatever has happened to the piano can be easily repaired," Clouseau explained with utmost patience. "Whatever has happened to Professor Fassbender and his poor daughter with the overdrawn bank account is a different matter, and it is my sworn duty to bring the guilty party or parties to justice. Now, so far, what do

38

we know? One, that Professor Fassbender and his daughter have been kidnapped. Two, that somebody kidnapped them. Three, that my hand is on fire!"

Clouseau howled in agony and plunged his red-hot gauntlet into a tank of tropical fish, creating an instant bouillabaisse. The smell of boiled fish suddenly filled the room. Superintendent Quinlan walked into the living room, having just driven out from London. "What in the name of God are you doing, Clouseau?" he asked.

Clouseau stood to one side of the room, energetically swinging his burned hand, which still held the flail, in a vain effort to create a cooling breeze. Before he could answer, Clouseau swung the flail through the glass doors of a gun cabinet containing several shot guns and rifles as well as a considerable supply of ammunition and a handsome pair of Navy duelling pistols. A twenty-gauge shotgun, full choke, fell out onto the floor, discharging both barrels and destroying the room.

10

Sir George Mercader, M.D., took a firm grip on the magnifying glass he held in his left hand. Then he sighed, picked up a sterilized pair of tweezers with his right hand, and returned to his patient. Dr. Mercader had spent the past twenty minutes digging number 2 birdshot out of the gluteus maximus of Superintendent Quinlan. "How do you feel?" the doctor inquired of his patient.

"My ass hurts." Quinlan winced. "And if you don't mind, let's not have any bad jokes about getting the lead out. I'm suffering enough as it is."

"Which reminds me," noted Drummond, who had driven his wounded partner direct to the doctor's Harley Street offices, "hunting season starts tomorrow."

"Maybe for you," Quinlan groaned, as Sir George dug out another pellet. "I feel like a bloody grouse. I don't suppose I'll be able to go bird shooting again."

"Hold still!" roared Sir George, who had been summoned from his club in the dead of night and was in a foul mood. The surgeon went deep after another lead pellet. Beads of sweat broke out on Quinlan's brow.

"Try to think of something pleasant," Drummond suggested.

"That's easy," the patient retorted. "Killing Clouseau would be the nicest thing I could imagine right about now."

Quinlan lay on his stomach on an examining table. He was covered with a sheet. Only his head and buttocks were exposed. A nurse stood abeam of Quinlan's rear quarters, holding a pan into which Sir George deposited the bits of ore he was mining in the Superintendent's living flesh. Occasionally the nurse would swab Quinlan's raw bum with a wad of cotton soaked in alcohol.

"Sister!" gasped Quinlan. "Why don't we give up and try for gangrene? I'm sure it'd be less painful."

"Silenzio," ordered Sir George's nurse, who was of Italian descent and had the mustache to prove it. The long-suffering Quinlan turned his attention back to Alec Drummond.

"Couldn't you just tell Paris that Clouseau's incompetent and request that he be taken off the case?"

Drummond admitted that the suggestion was indeed a tempting one. "How," he asked, "are we to avoid a serious diplomatic break with France if we presume to suggest that their greatest living detective is a fool?"

Quinlan tried hard not to think of what a sizable pain in the ass Sir George was becoming. "Are you absolutely positive we have the right Clouseau? The same chap who recovered the Pink Panther?"

Drummond nodded glumly and confessed he had even gone so far as to have Clouseau's fingerprints checked. There was, he admitted, no doubt as to the French detective's identity.

"Then that does it." Quinlan beamed. "Now I know what to do with my vacation! If old Clouseau's the best they've got, it's off to Paris for me and a life of crime. By the way, what's the bugger up to now?"

Drummond replied that Clouseau had taken up a round-the-clock stakeout at the Fassbender farm. Sir George looked up. "For God's sake, why?" Quinlan pointed to his bare bottom in silent rebuke and pleaded with Harley Street's finest surgeon to keep his mind on what he was doing.

"Clouseau suspects one of the staff," Drummond explained. "He thinks the butler did it."

Sir George Mercader slapped Quinlan smartly on the rump. "Good night, young man," he put on his dinner jacket back on. "The next time somebody decides to take a shot at you, please see to it that you apply to the National Health." And Sir George returned to his club.

Quinlan tried to get up but the nurse pushed him down again and liberally dusted his bottom with an antiseptic powder. Drummond could not stifle a laugh.

"Now what's so funny?" Quinlan demanded.

"If you don't mind my saying so, old boy," Drummond said through a chuckle, "you look like sunset over the Alps."

In Hartfordshire the rain had stopped and now a full moon shone down on the Fassbender farm. An owl hooted. Clouseau, crouched and stiff from his vigil behind a bracken hedge, shifted his weight and knelt on a sleeping cat. The cat sank its fangs into Clouseau's calf.

In the servant's quarters a light went out. A door opened. Jarvis emerged, looked around to make certain he was unobserved, and hurried across the cobblestoned car park to the garage. Jarvis put on his crash helmet and driving gloves and then pulled the tarpaulin off a vintage three-wheeler motorcycle complete with sidecar. Jarvis kicked the starter, gunned the throttle, and eased his bike up the driveway and onto the road to Barnet.

Clouseau slipped to the far side of the hedge. He momentarily caught his trousers on a branch. There was the sound of cloth tearing and then Clouseau was into his car and, with headlights off, in pursuit of Jarvis.

The drive took pursuer and quarry through the lovely, sleeping hamlet of Barnet and then west toward ancient St. Albans, where Jarvis parked his motorbike at the foot of the tenth-century Norman stone tower and entered a club called the Queen of Hearts.

Clouseau, driving without lights, missed the St. Albans turnoff and was halfway on the road to Aylesbury when he discovered his mistake. Only sheer good luck brought him cruising back through St. Albans. In truth, Clouseau had given up the search and was trying to find his way back to his London hotel when he spotted Jarvis's motorcycle parked in the shadows. Clouseau slammed on his brakes and backed up to a parking slot beside the Norman tower, dislodging several of the granite stones in the process.

Now what? Clouseau, unsure of his next move, pricked up his ears at the subdued sound of music coming from across the road. Clouseau approached a cabaret door over which burned a single roseate light. The name of the place was the Queen of Hearts and a carefully positioned sign advised one and all that this was an establishment "For Members Only." Clouseau, who would have ignored the sign had he seen it, walked through the door and into the murky, dimly lit interior of the Queen of Hearts.

The decor was early linoleum. There was a lot of fake red velvet and mirror. The bar was long and low and smelly. A black pianist played very bad jazz. Chuck, the headwaiter, lingered in the shadows idly picking his teeth. Couples in booths ringing the tiny dance floor bent low over guttering candles and minded their own business. At sight of Clouseau, Chuck took the toothpick from his mouth, wiped it off, and put it back in his pocket.

42

Chuck accosted Clouseau. "Yes?"

"Who are you?" Chuck strained to see through the gloom. "Or should I say, Where are you?"

"Over here." Chuck bumped Clouseau's elbow. "Didn't you see the sign 'Members Only'?"

Clouseau whipped out his official identification, which it was too dark to read. "I did not see your stupid sign. I do not believe in stupid signs. I am Chief Inspector Jacques Clouseau of the Sûreté and I am here on official business."

"How exciting," Chuck murmured.

"If you do not mind, I will have a look around," Clouseau whispered conspiratorially. "And I caution you: Do not breathe a word of my presence to your customers."

Chuck nodded. Clouseau could not even see Chuck's head.

"Who's the toff?" a strange voice—the bartender's —spoke up inches from Clouseau's ear.

"French cop," Chuck said through a yawn. "Pay him no mind and draw me a Guinness, there's a love."

From the recesses of the Queen of Hearts a single spotlight suddenly came on, blinding Clouseau. "Show time," announced a voice backstage. Clouseau groped his way to a ringside table and sat down on the lap of a woolens saleslady from Aberdeen and her escort. "Sorry," Clouseau mumbled, upsetting the woman's drink and finding the next table vacant. Clouseau was so grateful to be out of the hated limelight he did not even mind the fact that he was sitting in the puddle caused by the woman's spilled drink.

At the keyboard, "Magic Fingers" fumbled his way through an arpeggio. Then you could have heard a pin drop in the Queen of Hearts.

"Ladies and gentlemen," hissed the piano player, "once again it is my extreme joy and pleasure to introduce the incomparable . . . Ainsley Jarvis!"

Clouseau's deadly enemy, the hated spotlight, came on, once again blinding him. He was unable to recognize the Jarvis who minced out from backstage to the tiny dance floor. Jarvis wore a beautifully coiffured wig and a reasonable copy of a Givenchy gown. He began to sing in a husky, sensuous contralto.

In spite of himself, Clouseau began to experience a tiny tingling in his groin. For the moment he forgot about Jarvis and gave himself up to the enjoyment of the song and the singer. Jarvis moved among the tables, patting an arm here, a cheek there. "What's a Queen without a castle?" he sang.

At the back of the room, the Fassbender Kidnappers entered behind Chuck and looked around. Clouseau's attention remained riveted on the entertainer. A slight frown crossed his brow. There was something vaguely familiar about the big, attractive woman with the lovely voice.

"No Queen at all," sang Jarvis, who had spotted the Kidnappers the moment they had come into the Queen of Hearts. "And you'd be right again to say, winter's day is cold till you call." Slowly, Jarvis made his/her way to Clouseau's table and, horror of horrors, actually sat down on the same banquette. Clouseau turned bright pink and did his best to look suave.

Behind him the two Fassbender Kidnappers grabbed Chuck. One of the men did something to a nerve. Chuck folded up. The other man placed Chuck in the back of the coat closet. As the song soared to a graceful coda, the Fassbender Kidnappers resumed their scrutiny of the room and its patrons. Applause burst out on all sides. Jarvis handed the mike to a waiter, leaned back, and fluttered his false eyelashes at Clouseau.

Clouseau managed a weak smile. "I am not without some expertise in the performing arts," he announced, "and I must tell you, my dear, that you have a lovely, if somewhat untrained voice."

The singer smiled in appreciation. "How nice of you to say so, Jacques."

Clouseau's eyes widened. He leaned forward for a closer look into eyes that were of the deepest blue and surrounded by tiny blood vessels. "You . . . you're

44

Jarvis," Clouseau stammered. "What are you doing in a dress?"

"Making two hundred a week." Jarvis beamed. "What are you doing in a suit?"

Clouseau glanced about wildly. "I want to know why this afternoon you were Jarvis the Fassbenders' butler and tonight you are . . . you are . . ."

Clouseau found it difficult to go on, the more so because Jarvis had taken Clouseau's hand in his own and was kissing it tenderly. "I warn you," Clouseau said in a strangled voice as the bouncer came up to the table. Clouseau hastily yanked his hand away and leaped to his feet. Across the room the two Kidnappers looked in his direction.

"Something wrong, Ainsley?" growled the bouncer.

Jarvis shook his beautifully coiffured head. *"Por nada,* Bruno. The Inspector was just warning me to watch my step. You see, in France, he's known as the last tango in Paris."

"Tango?" bleated Clouseau, hopelessly lost in the small talk.

"Love to." Jarvis stood up and stepped into Clouseau's arms as the piano player sailed into a wretched medley with the aid of a trap drummer and a violinist who doubled as dishwasher.

"Wait!" protested Clouseau, unaware of the Kidnappers closing in. "I'd rather die than dance with you!"

"That, pet, is the choice," beamed Jarvis. And he made it look like Clouseau was doing the leading. They danced in silence, cheek to cheek, for a few bars. "You know," Jarvis murmured, "you're a very good dancer for a policeman."

Clouseau essayed a dip. "You are my first dancing butler," he admitted.

"I'll bet you tell that to all the butlers," Jarvis flirted. "My dressing room is through the curtains at the end of the hall. Quickly!"

"What are you suggesting?" protested Clouseau.

Jarvis pulled Clouseau close. "Don't look. They're coming this way."

Clouseau was baffled. "Who is coming which way?" The Larger Kidnapper tapped Clouseau on the shoulder. Jarvis and Clouseau kept dancing. Jarvis then clamped a strong grip on the back of Clouseau's neck, thereby preventing him from turning his head.

"You don't understand," grated the Larger Kidnapper. "I'm cutting in. And I'm not too particular who I'm cutting in on!" The Larger Kidnapper grabbed Jarvis and twisted him away from Clouseau.

"Rape!" screamed Jarvis. Clouseau shoved the Larger Kidnapper and was slugged in turn by his partner. Bruno waded into the fray, a roll of coins in each fist. Waiters piled into the brawl. Patrons screamed. Magic Fingers tried to hide under his stool. Somebody threw a bottle. Somebody else threw a chair. Somebody else picked up a table for four and threw it. A window was smashed. In the distance, a police siren wailed.

By dawn's early light, Alec Drummond was sitting with both feet up on his desk looking at a front-page photograph in the *Daily Express*. The three-column cut showed Clouseau and Jarvis being approached by half a dozen bobbies. "Still think I ought to call Paris?" Drummond queried.

Quinlan, who was standing by the window under the framed portrait of Princess Anne and Captain Mark and their jumpers, thought about that for a long time. "Look at it this way," he said at last. "I don't suppose it can get any worse. Can it?"

11

According to ancient Teutonic legend, Mondschein Castle was inspired by Attila the Hun, built by the illegitimate son-in-law of Ivan the Terrible, and occupied for more than three centuries by the Barbarian family. Maximilian Friedrich von Barbarian (the official family name) was a mild sort, given to rape and pillage, but only on holidays. It was his twin sons, Mad Rudi and his crazy brother Heinrich, who gave the family the bad name that has clung to them throughout history.

It was Rudi who, on Christmas Eve in 1537, turned to Heinrich and reportedly said, "To hell with waiting until tomorrow! I'm in the mood for rape tonight, dear brother. Are you with me?" Heinrich was already halfway to the stables to saddle the horses.

That night Rudi and Heinrich plowed their way through the maidens of all the villages lying within the shadow of Mondschein Castle, which in those days covered the equivalent of five counties. Thereafter, to their neighbors, the inhabitants of Mondschein Castle came to be known as "those goddamned Barbarians." The name stuck.

When the last of the von Barbarians, Siegfried the Simple, died in bed at the ripe old age of twelve, Mondschein Castle crumbled into disuse. It stood vacant (some claimed the place was haunted but that was so much hogwash) until a grandson of the first cousin of the nephew of the mistress of Frederick of Prussia took over the ancient ruin and restored it.

A local pretzel baron who stood four feet four and weighed over two hundred pounds, Wee Willi Wilder, dug the moat and added the crenelated battlements. In later years Wilder restored the torture chambers and solarium, added the drawbridge, and, at great cost, had a massive Wurlitzer organ hauled piece by piece up the steep sides of the Kreigenschaft Gorge by pack goats and installed in the music room.

From that day to the present, every time organ music was heard from the castle, the good burghers (and the bad burghers) of the valley below trembled in their shoes, for organ music at Mondschein Castle invariably meant bad juju.

The new owner of Mondschein Castle sat at the Wilder organ, playing happily. Charles Dreyfus, French ex-detective and former superior of Jacques Clouseau, had purchased Mondschein Castle for a song. When the ancient pile of Gothic ruins was put up for back taxes, so chilling was its reputation that there were no other bidders.

A creative man, Dreyfus had added homey, personal touches of his own. Such as the "Trespassers Will Be Shot" signs, the electric fences, floodlights, and machine-gun mounts on the parapets that overlooked the entire valley and even caused a modicum of concern in nearby Berchtesgaden, where Dreyfus initially had gone castle hunting but had been turned away with a curt "We got noddings for sale herein."

Dreyfus was in a beautiful mood. He let his fingers wander over the keyboard. In the lush Valley of the Lederkranz below, farmers looked up from their haying as the strains of "Sweet Leilani" and "Tiptoe Through the Tulips," as well as other oldies but goodies, filtered down from above.

When Dreyfus sequed to "Muskrat Ramble," a cow in the Widow Hourlimann's barn swiftly gave birth to a two-headed calf. The calf thereupon turned on its mother and bit her, twice.

Suddenly all music stopped. In Mondschein Castle, Cairo Fred and Tournier the Bank Robber led Dr. Fassbender and his daughter Margo into the music room. The Fassbenders were blindfolded and manacled. They had stood bravely facing the music, until the mad organist abruptly terminated his concert halfway through "The Folks Who Live on the Hill."

Dreyfus, his mad eye twitching in anticipation, instructed Cairo Fred to untie the Fassbenders. Even before blood circulation had been restored to Fassbender's arms, Dreyfus was pumping his hand most warmly. "Professor Fassbender," he purred. "What an honor to have you and your lovely daughter as my guests."

"Who the devil are you?"

Cairo Fred, who had neglected to remove the blindfolds, now did so.

Dreyfus cackled appreciatively. "Who the devil indeed! Ha-ha-ha! That is a good one! Let us just say, for the moment, that I am your host. I will do everything in my power to make your stay here in Mondschein Castle as pleasant as possible . . . providing, of course, that you reciprocate by giving me something that I want very much."

Fassbender steeled himself for what was to follow. "And that would be?"

Margo eyed her father adoringly. How brave he stood! And how fearless! If only he had not been cursed with incurable dandruff.

Dreyfus rambled on, expressing his keen admiration for Fassbender's breakthrough in top-security work for the British Government in the field of time-space relationships and related matters that were said to be beyond the ken of an Einstein.

"I am particularly fascinated by what you have done in the area of vortices of electromagnetic aberrations."

A shudder went through Fassbender. "I see." He wet his lips. "And do you work for a particular foreign government, or do you expect to sell my discovery to the highest bidder?"

Cairo Fred and Tournier exchanged uneasy glances. The Old Man was not accustomed to putting up with this kind of shit from his captives. But Dreyfus continued as though nothing out of the ordinary had happened.

He led Professor Fassbender into the new wing of Mondschein Castle, where a modern, fully equipped laboratory had just been installed. Fassbender stared unbelievingly at the expensive equipment, which must have cost several fortunes and was far more sophisticated than anything he had seen before.

"We are about to join forces, you and I." As Dreyfus explained his project, blood vessels in his temples pumped until they seemed about to burst. "We shall conquer the world! Dibs on North America," Dreyfus concluded.

Margo Fassbender, who was not given to displays of emotion, promptly burst into tears.

"You're mad," the Professor observed.

Dreyfus danced a little jig in front of the giant computer bank. "Mad? Was Hannibal mad? And Alexander? Surely Napoleon was the maddest of them all!" Saliva dribbled down Dreyfus's chin.

Fassbender drew himself up to his full six feet seven inches. "I shall tell you nothing," he promised.

"Attaboy, Daddy," whispered Margo.

"*Au contraire,* as we say in the old country," grinned Dreyfus. "I think you will give me your full co-operation."

"I'll die first," said Fassbender calmly, in his very best Lawrence of Arabia manner. Not for nothing had he been known in his undergraduate days at Oxford as "King of the Clichés."

Dreyfus wasted no further time. He turned to Cairo Fred and said, "Show Miss Fassbender the schoolroom."

Cairo Fred began dragging Margo into the hall. The poor girl shrieked in terror. Fassbender struggled with Tournier. "You fiend!" he shouted at Dreyfus.

"Why not show Professor Fassbender your razor trick," Dreyfus suggested as he went out after Cairo Fred and Margo Fassbender. Tournier whipped out a hand-tooled Harlem special and pressed it against the Professor's jugular vein. Fassbender sat down.

Cairo Fred was strapping Margo Fassbender into a chair as Dreyfus entered the schoolroom. Margo rolled her eyes in terror. "What are you going to do?"

"Something painful, you can be sure of that." Dreyfus promised. "Something so hideous that your father will have no choice but to co-operate with me."

Margo pleaded for mercy. Dreyfus stepped to a Louis Quinze table and opened a porcelain box containing cotton, which he began stuffing into his ears. Tournier followed suit. Only then did Dreyfus step to the blackboard. He raised a clawlike hand, his eyes glittering in Satanic fury. Margo stiffened, then screamed as Dreyfus scraped his fingernails across the blackboard again and again.

Across the great hall, in the laboratory, Professor Fassbender buried his head in his hands as his daughter's screams tore through the castle. "All right" Fassbender knew Margo was a fragile child. "Enough! Get Dreyfus! I'll tell him everything!"

Tournier stepped across the hall into the schoolroom. Abruptly Margo's screams stopped.

12

It was Saturday afternoon. On the White House lawn squirrels chattered in the October sunlight. In the Oval Office the red telephone had been taken off its stand. The "Do Not Disturb" sign hung in its accustomed place on the door. The President was watching a football game.

Flanked by a U.S. Admiral, the Senior Senator from Virginia, and the Secretary of State, the President sat in front of a television set and watched the young men of the University of Michigan and the U.S. Naval Academy try to do terrible things to each other. In the background, aides to the various VIP's assembled made bets on the outcome of the game. In the stadium at Ann Arbor, the Navy Band played "Anchors Aweigh" as the host Michigan bandsmen courteously tried to drown them out with the Wolverine fight song. It was time-out on the playing field in what everyone had to agree had been one hell of a football game. Thanks to an early, first-quarter touchdown, Navy led, 7 to 3. The Middies had the ball deep in their own territory with only seconds remaining.

"Michigan has to get the ball back in these waning moments of the game or we may be seeing the biggest upset of the season," commented the noted play-by-play announcer, Vin Scully.

"In a pig's eye!" The Chief Executive pounded his fist into his palm. "Come on, Michigan!"

"Go, Navy!" yelled the Admiral, for the moment forgetting where he was. The President turned slowly to glare.

"How would you like a transfer to the Gulf of Aden?"

Without waiting for an answer, the President turned his attention once again to the television screen. He smiled as a Navy running play lost a yard. "Sloppy! Sloppy!" grunted the Admiral.

"Calm yo'self, Jonas," offered the Virginia Senator. "It ain't nothin' but a game."

"Game, hell!" raged the Admiral. "This is war!"

The Oval Office crackled with tension as Navy went into punt formation. Upfield the Michigan safetyman nervously spat into his hands and squinted into the slanting rays of the sun. The kick came his way, a beautiful, high-arching spiral.

The Michigan safety man drifted back, back under the ball, gathered it in smoothly, and took off on a long, twisting run upfield. "Go, Aronowitz!" yelled the President. The Admiral came out of his chair. "Get the little son of a bitch!" he screamed. "Kill him!"

David Aronowitz ran as though his life and his scholarship depended on it. He crossed midfield and twisted and fought his way to the Navy nine-yard line. The Michigan stands went wild.

The President challenged the Admiral. "A hundred shares of oil stock says they score."

The sportscaster chattered into his mike. "Well, folks, here it is! The chips are on the line! The fat's in the fire! And the lowing herd winds slowly o'er the lea! Michigan has used up all of its time-outs—or is it times-out? Anyway, there is only time enough for one more play!"

The President leaned forward tensely. So did the Admiral. The Secretary of State, who did not understand American football, thought momentarily of going to the bathroom but quickly decided against it. The Senator licked his lips. On the nine-yard line Navy dug in determinedly. Michigan went into its set position. "Flanker left," the sportscaster dutifully reported. "A man in motion . . ."

Suddenly the picture went dead and was replaced almost immediately by a full head shot of Charles Dreyfus. He was smiling wildly, his eye twitching a mile a minute.

"What happened?" the President yelled. "Where's the game?" Frantically he grabbed the remote control and began switching channels. Dreyfus was on every station—grinning like a madman on CBS, simpering on NBC, dribbling spit on ABC.

"Who is that nut?" Kissel inquired.

"The man seems to be on every channel," the Senator observed sagely.

"Call the FCC," roared the President. The Oval Office was in an uproar. Nothing quite like it had been seen since the Cuban Missile Crisis.

"I think he's trying to say something," said the Senator from Virginia.

"Calm down, everybody," said the Secretary of State who was a good hand at this sort of thing.

"Calm down, hell!" yelled the President. "Did Michigan score?"

"Maybe we ought to hear what the fellow has to say." The Senator was beginning to make a nuisance of himself. Gradually the tumult in the room began to subside. All eyes were on the television screen.

". . . little enough to ask," Dreyfus was saying. "The life of one man against the holocaust that could destroy the globe."

"What in hell's he talking about?" demanded the Admiral.

The President raised his hand. "Quiet." On TV Dreyfus rambled on, growing more agitated by the moment. "That is why I say again, give me Clouseau and we can all sleep secure in our beds."

The President scowled at his Secretary of State. "What's a Clouseau?"

"Sure beats me," offered the Admiral. "Say, what's wrong with that fellow's eye?"

"Did he say something about destroying the globe?" asked the Secretary of State. "That could be important."

"Hush," said the Senator and thought about baked ham.

Dreyfus was nearing the end of his little fireside chat. ". . . and so, next week, I am prepared to give the world a demonstration of the awesome power I hold. On Saturday, October thirtieth at precisely three P.M. Eastern Standard Time, the United Nations Building in New York City will vanish from the face of the earth. Thank you for your attention and good night." Dreyfus's image vanished.

The telecast from Michigan Stadium came back on. The picture showed a scene of pandemonium. Crowds of spectators swarmed over the playing field. The game has just ended. Goal posts were being torn down.

The President looked as though he wanted to cry. "Get the FBI, the CIA, the Pentagon," he ordered. Aides leaped to a battery of telephones. "For God's sake, find out who won the damn game!!"

Three thousand miles away, on the other side of the Atlantic, Alec Drummond handed Quinlan a sheet of paper. "That's a photograph taken while the broadcast was in progress," he commented. "A Japanese student took it with a Leica."

Quinlan studied the photograph of Dreyfus. "Do I know him?"

Drummond nodded. "Paris identified him as one Charles Dreyfus . . . former Chief Inspector of the Sûreté."

"I can't believe it," said Quinlan, who had a history of being difficult.

"Let me go on reading the report," Drummond pleaded. "Where was I? Oh, yes . . . Dreyfus. More recently, an inmate at the State Mental Health Facility for the Criminally Insane at Aix-Aux-Deux until he escaped." Drummond passed over a second sheet of paper. "Here's a text of what he said on the telly. He obviously controls equipment sophisticated enough to pirate the communications satellite whenever he feels inclined."

Quinlan's lips moved as he read the Dreyfus transcription. "Give me Clouseau and we can all sleep secure in our beds'?" He looked up at Drummond.

"I thought you'd find that interesting," grunted his colleague.

"One crazy Chief Inspector talking about another crazy Chief Inspector. What do you think he means by 'give me Clouseau'? And listen to this." He read on: " ' . . . little enough to ask, the life of one man, against the holocaust'."

"I believe he also made some threat about making the UN Building disappear," Drummond reminded.

"Crikey!" Quinlan suddenly smacked his own forehead with his palm. "Operation Looking-Glass!"

Drummond's face went white. "Fassbender!" he blurted. Drummond flipped on his intercom. "Get me Lovell at the Home Office!"

Drummond faced Quinlan. "Where's Clouseau?"

13

The four-story Hotel Grouse-Moor on London's Cromwell Road could best be described as one half fleabag and one half flytrap. Its clientele leaned toward retired madams, Pakistani medical students and unemployed disk jockeys. The lift was unsafe and the kitchen atrocious. Yet to men like Clouseau the Grouse-Moor represented a kind of home away from home.

Eyes constantly sweeping both sides of the busy Cromwell Road for activities of a suspicious nature, the gifted detective bounced energetically into the shabby little lobby and up to the desk. Rounders, the clerk, was on duty. He glared at Clouseau, who banged his hand up and down on his bell. Up and down.

"You have a massage for me?" inquired Clouseau politely.

"You want a massage?" asked Rounders. "At this time of day?"

"If you have one for me, yes," said the beaming Clouseau, who did not even mind the clerk's celebrated halitosis. Rounders had been permanently barred from the Regents Park Zoo since the day he hiccoughed in the birdhouse and wiped out a family of coots, six emperor penguins and a ptarmigan.

"Why don't you try Little Tokyo at the end of the block?" asked Rounders, whose feet were beginning to itch despite his meticulous habit of changing his socks at least once a month. "Ask for Passion Flower Shirley, the Yokohama Butterfly," he added helpfully.

Clouseau had a hard time figuring out that particular gratuitous piece of information. "Why should I ask for Passion Shirley, the Yakamama Butterball?"

"You said you wanted a massage." Rounders was trying to be patient, although he found it becoming increasingly difficult.

"Yes," shot back Clouseau. "But from you!"

Rounders was offended, since he did not give massages and had no intention of starting now with Clouseau.

"But you gave me one only this morning!" Clouseau insisted with maddening persistence. "The massage was from Superintendent Quinlan from the Yard of Scotland!"

Somewhere in the dim recesses of Rounders's skull a light flickered on. The French idiot standing in front of him had kept saying "massage" in the mistaken belief that he was pronouncing the word message. Rounders secretly cursed the Eiffel Tower and French pastry.

"Well?" Clouseau began drumming on the desk. "Do you or do you not have for me the massage?"

Rounders made a great show of searching his message file. Then he turned back to Clouseau and smiled hatefully. For Clouseau there was no message. "And if you continue to hang about my desk," said Rounders, his patience practically gone, "I'll breathe on you! I swear I will!"

Clouseau backed across the lobby to the lift, which happened to be working on this particular day. As the ancient cage bore him upstairs, the switchboard buzzed behind Rounders. The clerk plugged in. "Hotel Grouse-Moor. Good evening . . . Inspector Clouseau? He just went up to his room. I'll ring." Rounders depressed the "ring" key.

The telephone in room 43 rang loudly for a very long time. It stopped ringing as Clouseau unlocked the door and strode into his domain, which consisted of one iron bed, one canvas chair, a leaky wash basin, and privileges to the community loo on the third floor. A vague telephonic vibration in the air made Clouseau life the phone, which was attached to the wall just inside the door, between it and the only window.

Clouseau had just picked up the phone and kicked the door shut behind him when it was opened immediately by the night maid, a rather large, muscular young woman from Uganda. The opening of the door swept Clouseau out the window, where he dangled, three stories above Cromwell Road, the telephone still grasped in his hand.

"Hello!" Clouseau shouted. "Hello!" There was no answer. Clouseau began pulling himself back up the telephone line, hand over hand.

In the room the night maid had just finished turn-

appeared in the open window behind her. The night maid exited, forgetting her large ring of room keys, ing down the bed when Clouseau's contorted features which she left on the bed. Unfortunately for Clouseau, remembrance returned to the night maid literally as he was pulling himself in through the window. Bang! went the door as the night maid opened it roughly again. Zoom! went Clouseau out the window. Scoop! went the night maid sweeping her keys off the bed. Slam! went the door.

A Clouseau fooled once cannot be fooled again. Surmising that some sort of fiendish assassination plot was taking place in room 43, Clouseau thought to save his life and a good bit of needless climbing by pulling himself through the window of room 33. Clouseau's timing could not have been better. He reached the sill just as the night runner from Uganda burst into room 33 and knocked Clouseau ass over attaché case out the window once again. In room 43 the telephone installation began to come out of the wall as the pull of dead weight on the line continued.

In the lobby, Rounders was seated before his switchboard, trying to pick tomorrow's winners at Haydock. Suddenly the entire switchboard was yanked through the wall, dragging Rounders with it by his headset. Pieces of plaster cascaded down on the room clerk. Clouseau, looking very much like he had been run over by a convoy of trucks on a highway, staggered into the lobby from outside still holding his room telephone.

Rounders weakly shoved a scrap of paper toward Clouseau. "Your message," he hissed.

Clouseau laid his room phone on what was left of the reception desk. "Thank you," with a polite bow. "And here is your phone!"

Swiftly Clouseau's eyes scanned the message. "Come at once! Have I got a clue for you!" The message was signed "Ainsley Jarvis." Clouseau charged out into the middle of Cromwell Road, where he was almost run down by a double-decker bus. He grabbed the nearest, and only, taxicab on the street. Clouseau jumped into the back seat and shouted a St. Albans address to the driver.

Twenty minutes later the ancient taxi was still wheezing its way along Cromwell Road toward the Hammersmith Flyover. Clouseau leaned forward and tapped the elderly driver's shoulder. "Can't you go any faster?" he pleaded.

"Not unless we stop off at my flat and pick up my Ferrari," rasped the driver. Clouseau gritted his teeth and sank back against the seat cushions.

By dint of some reckless driving, the taxi man was able to deposit his passenger outside the Queen of Hearts just as the eleven o'clock show was about to start. Clouseau found a table as Magic Fingers the piano player mangled a tremolo.

"And now, ladies and gentlemen . . . once again it is my profound and unctuous pleasure to present the incomparable . . . Ainsley Jarvis!" Patrons applauded. The drummer played a drum roll. Clouseau craned to see Ainsley's entrance. Nothing happened. The piano player essayed another tremolo, this one better than the first. "Like I said before, Ainsley Jarvis!" he said mincingly. Again the star performer failed to answer his cue. "Must be a zipper stuck somewhere," observed the piano player, going for a laugh and deservedly getting stares.

Clouseau got up and headed backstage, where he knocked tentatively at the door to the lone dressing room. He was answered by a groan. Clouseau kicked in the door, despite the fact that it was unlocked. Sprawled on the floor lay Ainsley Jarvis, beside him a thoroughly dead Kidnapper. The tiny cubicle was a shambles of spilled sequins, mascara, and false eyelashes. Clouseau knelt beside Jarvis. He felt for some sign of a pulse. Jarvis seemed to be trying to say something. Clouseau leaned closer to hear, putting his ear beside the dying man's lips. With a final effort, Jarvis turned his head, kissed Clouseau full on the mouth, and died.

A shadow fell across Clouseau. Superintendent Quinlan and Section Director Drummond stood in the doorway behind him. Quinlan looked accusingly at Clouseau. "Why didn't you try to give him the kiss of life?" asked the man from Scotland Yard.

"Because at that very instant he was giving me the kiss of death," Clouseau explained. "I liked old Jarvis—but not in the way that you think!" Clouseau added quickly.

Quinlan and Drummond went through the dead man's personal effects. "He said or did nothing before he died?" Clouseau shook his head as Section Director McLaren hurried into the room, which was getting rather crowded. McLaren handed Quinlan the coroner's report.

"Amazing. Even after Jarvis had been stabbed twice, he was still able to break the Kidnapper's neck."

"What is so amazing about that?" Clouseau could not understand all the fuss.

"Amazing that the coroner was able to type up a report before he got back to the Yard," said Quinlan. "This new coroner is a gung-ho laddie!" Quinlan got to his feet. "Might as well go back to the Yard. Chances are we won't find anything here." He started to leave. Clouseau plucked at Quinlan's sleeve.

"Don't you want to see my clue?" Clouseau held out the travel brochure the dying Jarvis had pressed into his hand.

"What's this?" Quinlan scanned the brochure disinterestedly.

"A travel brochure advertising the Oktoberfest in Munich," Clouseau explained. "It begins the day after tomorrow." Clouseau beamed on one and all. "The case is practically solved."

"Just because you think the dead man was planning to go there, perhaps to meet someone? Come on, Clouseau! That's a bit much . . . even for you."

Clouseau unlocked his attaché case and took out several files until he found what he was looking for. It was a photograph of Charles Dreyfus, taken in dress uniform when he was Chief Inspector of the

Sûreté. It was inscribed: "To my partner in the war against crime, Charles."

Clouseau chewed reflectively at one corner of the photograph, his mind working overtime. "Partners in the war against crime . . . and now . . . arch enemies," he mused. "Nature plays funny tricks."

"You need help," Drummond opined.

Clouseau disagreed. "I prefer to do this alone, if you don't have any objection."

Quinlan sided with Drummond against Clouseau. "If Dreyfus is what we suspect he is, he has an army behind him."

Clouseau shrugged and allowed a modest smile to play at the corners of his mouth. It was something he had been practicing for weeks and he did it very well. "Oh, it won't be easy," Clouseau allowed. "But then nothing worthwhile ever is. That is why I have always failed where others have succeeded. For me, the greater the odds, the greater the challenge. And, as always, I choose to accept the challenge. Gentlemen, good night! I am off to Munich!"

So saying, Clouseau turned and marched into the closet. He reappeared almost immediately. "Very ingenious. For a moment you nearly had me fooled. It is your good fortune that I was not looking for the men's room!"

Drummond and Quinlan watched Clouseau walk out the correct door this time and into the night. A taxi door slammed. "I think we ought to call Germany and warn them," Drummond suggested.

"About Dreyfus?" asked Quinlan.

"About Clouseau," Drummond said wincing. "As far as history is concerned, one lunatic like that let loose in a beer hall was enough!"

61

14

On October 30, the President called an emergency meeting of his Cabinet, plus the Joint Chiefs of Staff and the top men from the C.I.A., the F.B.I., and the Secret Service. A bank of television monitors, which had been installed in the Oval Room, offered panoramic views of the entire area surrounding the United Nations Building in Manhattan.

Just now the cameras showed empty streets and sidewalks for half a mile in every direction around the world-famous structure. Along the East River, National Guard roadblocks effectively stopped all vehicular traffic. Bridges had been closed. Navy patrol boats and a newly commissioned submarine cruised offshore, while overhead seven helicopters and a squadron of jet fighters from Mitchell Field kept the skies clear of would-be saboteurs and terrorists.

"Tightest security I've ever seen," said the President, acknowledging his appreciation to the nation's peace-keeping forces. "I don't think a gnat could get inside the UN Building."

He glanced at his watch. The little hand was almost on the three, the big hand just approaching the twelve. "Five minutes to go," said the President.

"Two," corrected the Secretary of Commerce, who was not destined to remain in his job for very long.

"We're going to look like a bunch of assholes if this turns out to be a hoax," grunted the Admiral.

"We'd look a lot worse," shot back the President, "if we didn't take every precaution and it turned out *not* to be a hoax. Certainly Dr. Fassbender and Operation Looking-Glass are hardly your ordinary Halloween prank."

The Admiral ran a hand through thinning, silver

hair, which he rinsed each night with a bluing he pinched from his wife. "God—a weapon like that in the hands of a wacky Frenchman!"

Carstairs, of the CIA, sat bolt upright in his chair. The television monitor covering Franklin D. Roosevelt Drive showed a tiny moving object. "Hey!" he shouted. "What's that?"

The FBI Director, who had twenty-twenty vision, took a close look. "Relax." He smiled. "It's only somebody's dog."

In New York City the sun continued to shine down on skyscraper and tenement alike. But at Mondschein Castle, heavy rainclouds shrouded the turrets and the mountain freshet hurled itself against the gorge.

Giant generators hummed in the laboratory as Dr. Fassbender moved about among the machinery, making last-minute adjustments. Computer panel lights winked on and off. The Doomsday Machine, resembling a giant transparent telescope, rested on its platform directly beneath the hood of its silo. Dreyfus dogged the Professor's every move, eyes shining in unholy anticipation.

"Are you positive you can do it?" Dreyfus demanded for the forty-fourth time. He was starting to get on Fassbender's nerves.

"Theoretically, yes," the scientist speculated.

Dreyfus could not suppress a giggle. "For the sake of your daughter, I sincerely hope so. For should you fail"—here a cloud darker than those lowering outside crossed Dreyfus's brow—"I should have to do mean and evil things to poor little Margo."

The gaunt Professor was ashen-faced. "I have done everything you asked," he began. Dreyfus cut him off impatiently.

"Not yet! When the UN Building vanishes, *then* you will have done everything I asked and not until then." Dreyfus suddenly did a completely extemporaneous and thoroughly charming time step. "What do you suppose they will name the crater? Maybe the Dreyfus Ditch?"

63

Fassbender paused in the act of throwing a complicated series of switches. The nose of the Doomsday Machine swung from the tip of Baffin Bay south toward Long Island Sound. "There should be no crater," he intoned. "Not if my calculations are correct."

Dreyfus stamped his foot angrily. "But I want a crater!" he screamed. "Wreckage! Twisted metal! Something the world won't forget! Like Hiroshima!"

Fassbender was nearly ready. "The world has already forgotten Hiroshima," he noted sadly. "They will not forget today."

A shiver of anticipation ran through Dreyfus. "Good." He moved restlessly, almost hopping from toe to toe. "I have to pee again! Don't do anything till I get back!"

"Wet your pants," Fassbender suggested. "I have already started the countdown."

On United Nations Plaza, a small French poodle broke away from its owner and dashed off a few paces, pausing to lift its leg against the southwest corner of the UN Building. "Hey!" shouted a policeman. "You can't do that!" He struggled with the poodle's owner, a second-rate night club comic named Danny Salvo, which happened to be his real name.

"So what's the big deal?" cracked Salvo, King of the Catskills. "Since when is it against the law for a citizen to take a leak?"

The clock on the wall in the Oval Room showed thirty seconds.

In the laboratory at Mondschein Castle, Professor Fassbender continued the countdown. "Eight," he intoned, "seven . . . six . . . five . . . four . . ."

The generators hummed loudly. Computer reels kicked in. Dreyfus was practically having an orgasm. "Three," he squeaked. "Two . . . one . . . *Ignition!!!*"

The thin, needlelike nose of the Doomsday Machine glowed, hummed, whistled. The entire machine turned a luminescent puce. Stars fell on Alabama.

In New York City, before the horrified stares of millions of American television viewers, the United Nations Building began to turn a luminescent puce. So did Danny Salvo's poodle, particularly the dog's front half.

And then, inexplicably, the United Nations Building was gone. It simply vanished. And so did the forepart of the poodle. One moment there had been the commonplace sight of a dog urinating against a building. Now all that remained was the rear half of a pedigreed French poodle. Having relieved itself, the rear end of the dog hurried off happily.

On the Evening News, the disappearance of the United Nations Building was lead story.

"Good evening." The newscaster chose his words carefully. "The man who today made good his threat to eliminate the United Nations Building in New York has been identified by French Police sources. He is Charles Dreyfus, former Chief Inspector of the Sûreté and more recently an inmate in the French State Mental Health Facility for the Criminally Insane. But just how Dreyfus managed to carry out his daring boast remains shrouded in diplomatic and scientific secrecy."

The commentator fought to control a sudden tendency of his left hand to tremble as he turned toward camera 2. "The President," he continued smoothly, "has imposed a complete news blackout over today's dramatic events in New York; however, it is known now that no explosive device or bomb was used. The UN Building simply disappeared from its foundations, as though a giant hand had reached down from the sky and plucked it like a piece of ripe fruit."

The studio floor manager gave the newsman an expected cue. In the control room an assistant director flicked a switch, cutting in a remote unit that had been standing by.

"We take you now to the Hill Veterinary Hospital for an interview with Dr. Zelmo Flek, director of neurosurgery, and Mr. Danny Salvo, the owner of a dog named Shlep. A pedigreed miniature French poodle,

Shlep is the only known casualty of today's incredible series of events."

The television cameras cut to a rather startling picture of the interior of a hospital room. Between Danny Salvo and a beaming Dr. Flek sat Shlep, or, rather, one half of Shlep. All that was visible of Shlep were his hind legs, his tail, and the rear half of his torso. Shlep, who loved attention, wagged his tail frantically. Somehow, the commentator was able to continue his broadcast.

"Good evening, Dr. Flek." The newscaster's voice echoed eerily in the hospital room.

Dr. Flek looked around for the voice. "Good evening," he managed.

"How is your patient?" the interviewer continued. "Medically speaking, what is the condition of the dog?"

"Sound as a dollar," said Dr. Flek, "or should I say half-dollar?" Beside him Danny Salvo looked stricken. "I have made a series of exhaustive tests of the dog, or his available half, and I can find nothing wrong. Except that Shlep's head, heart, brain and lungs somehow seem to be missing. Other than that, Shlep is in perfect condition. His digestive system is functioning and his temperature is normal. We know Shlep is getting nourishment because the little bastard has crapped twice on the carpet in my office."

The censor who should have bleeped the offending words was too fascinated by sound and picture to make the electronic erasure. For the first time in history, two hundred million U.S. citizens heard the word crap on television. Somehow it seemed appropriate.

The newscaster directed his next question to Danny Salvo, who had been trying desperately to get on. "How does it feel to be the owner of half a dog?"

"Weird," quipped Danny. "I'm putting in for a refund for half the mutt's license. I was only joking. But seriously, who needs a dog that can't lick your hand or go fetch? And that's not the worst. You want to know what happened when I took Shlep home? I'll tell you what happened. The cat had a heart attack.

66

My wife went off the wagon. And the kids haven't stopped crying. The neighbors haven't quit laughing. I mean, how can you take something like that for a walk on a leash?" He gestured toward Shlep. "Even if you could, where would you fasten the leash?"

The cameras directed attention back to the veterinarian. "Obviously Shlep is feeling no pain," the commentator observed. "On the contrary, he seems to be quite happy. I notice his tail hasn't stopped wagging since we went on the air." Dr. Flek nodded sagely. "Where do you think Shlep's missing half is?" the interviewer asked, neatly serving the ball into Flek's court.

"I was talking to a colleague of mine, Dr. Hardpeg, about that very thing. Hardpeg examined Shlep this afternoon. Hardpeg is very smart. He told me that Shlep's missing half is in another dimension."

"Do you mean to say that the missing half of the dog is not dead, but alive and well?" the newsman probed.

"And functioning normally in every way, although of course we cannot see it," Dr. Flek assured him. "Shlep's missing half is invisible, that's all."

15

A Mercedes-Benz taxi drew up in front of the Hotel Bayerischerhof, one of Munich's finest hostelries. Clouseau got out, having learned the folly of economy by his experience at the Grouse-Moor. The cabdriver removed Clouseau's valise from the trunk and handed it to the hotel porter. Clouseau quickly snatched back the suitcase. "I never let this bag out of my sight," he explained.

The Bayerischerhof porter had held his position for nearly forty years and was accustomed to kooks. He shrugged and re-entered the lobby, where he stared at the cashier's legs. Clouseau set down his suitcase and turned to pay the driver. A second taxi pulled up in front of the Bayerischerof and ran over the suitcase. Clouseau sighed and picked up his battered valise. There was the sound of broken glass.

Clouseau walked into the lobby enveloped in a cloud of shaving lotion. His appearance was duly noted by the Fassbender Kidnapper, who had been lurking at the tobacco counter since early morning. At the desk Clouseau accepted his room key.

"I hope you enjoy your stay in Munich at the world-famous Oktoberfest, Inspector," said the clerk. *"Prosit."*

"I am not here to enjoy my stay," Clouseau explained confidentially. He wondered if all hotel clerks suffered from acute halitosis. This fellow could blow poor Rounders out of the water. Clouseau reached to pick up his suitcase only to find that a bellman had beaten him to it. The valise swung in the bellman's grip, giving off tinkling sounds. "Now see what you have done, you fool!" Clouseau glowered and snatched back the valise.

As he crossed to the lift, the Kidnapper picked up a pay telephone. He dialed a Bavarian number. In Mondschein Castle, Tournier picked up the telephone the instant it rang. "Clouseau has just gone up to his room," reported the Kidnapper.

Tournier glanced around, making sure he was not overheard. "Watch him. Don't let him out of your sight. Call me later," Tournier said quickly as Dreyfus sidled up behind him.

"Who was that?"

"Wrong number," Tournier grumbled. ·

Dreyfus linked arms with Tournier. It was almost time for his next telecast to the world. He needed Tournier upstairs in the control booth.

Manila's Corregidor Memorial Auditorium, site of this year's Miss Galaxy Beauty Contest, was jammed. Television cameras transmitted the pagan rites throughout the world, where they were accorded the attention worthy of a Second Coming.

At Polli's Truckers' Paradise outside Vineland, on U.S. 1, the regulars jostled with visiting Teamsters for space in front of the twenty-five-inch color TV set. No redball express would roll this night until the new Miss Galaxy had been introduced, ogled, and crowned.

In Manila the beauteous contestants were presented by a pompadored Master of Ceremonies with glistening teeth. A dedicated member of the Gay Community, he was ideal for the job, being the lone impartial member of the International Panel of Judges, whose members included three nobleman, five ambassadors, a soccer star, a band leader, and two plastic surgeons.

"Miss Iceland," crooned the Master of Ceremonies. A leggy blonde in a brief swimsuit surged forward. From Ogonquit to Oswego male hearts beat just a little faster.

"Lookit them shock absorbers," cried one of the truck connoisseurs at the bar. "Her transmission ain't bad either," noted his companion, a lady trucker driving a Diesel rig out of Duluth.

Miss Iceland finished her turn and bounced off into the wings. The Master of Ceremonies cleared his throat and waited for applause to die down. "Miss Great Britain!"

Cries of rage exploded as the image of Dreyfus filled the world's television screens. "Get him off!" screamed a driver, who was supposed to be delivering a truckload of rocket parts to Cape Kennedy.

A White House aide who had been watching the beauty pageant on his dinner break upset his drink and called the President's suite. The President was having dinner with members of his family, as well as the Secretary of State and his date for the evening. A Secret Service agent quickly turned on the TV set. Suddenly the image of Dreyfus filled the White House sets once again. The President nearly choked on a forkful of broccoli.

"Once again, my friends, good evening," Dreyfus was saying. "Today the UN Building, tomorrow . . . who knows?"

The Secretary of State's date, a Bennington graduate student, opened her lovely lips to make a comment. The President gestured her to silence.

"I presume that the nations of the world are duly impressed with the awesome power which I control," Dreyfus ranted on. "A power so great that, should I choose, I could wipe out an entire city . . . like Moscow."

In the Kremlin, faces around the NKVD black-and-white fifteen-inch television screen went pale.

"Or London," Dreyfus continued teasingly. At Number Ten Downing Street, the Prime Minister upset his breakfast kippers.

"Perhaps Paris," Dreyfus crowed. The bells of Notre Dame began pealing wildly in alarm.

"The lucky city might even be Washington, D.C."

By now Dreyfus was drunk with power. The President gulped a handful of antacid pills.

"What about Peking or Cairo, you maniac?" he shouted at the television screen.

"But why confine the destruction to a city?" Dreyfus artfully posed the question. "Why not an entire country? China, perhaps. Or Egypt!"

"That's more like it." The President beamed. His abdominal cramps subsided.

Dreyfus glanced fondly around the impromptu television studio he had installed in his wonderful castle. Ah, he thought. The things that money could buy! He smiled at the loyal henchmen sitting across the room from him: Cairo Fred, with the laughing face; Hindu Harry the Sniper, a mischievous killer with the conscience of a cobra; Bruce the Knife. They were his family now. How he loved them! As he continued with his telecast, a small lump rose in Dreyfus's throat.

"Of course," he went on smoothly, "the choice is up to you, my friends throughout the world. Hear my terms: within one week, if Chief Inspector

Jacques Clouseau is not dead, I shall be forced to select another target for my darling Doomsday Machine. The Vatican? A city? Why not a country? Even a continent! Think. I call on the nations of the world to co-operate in the common cause of self-preservation. Do I ask something so terrible?" Dreyfus paused for emphasis, then lowered his voice and spoke terribly slowly.

"It isn't as though this were the first time civilized countries have resorted to political assassination for less than valid reasons. For what is the life of one man . . . this man . . . this . . . menace . . . this nincompoop"—Dreyfus struggled for control—"compared with the loss of millions of innocent lives?" Dreyfus swallowed. Suddenly he felt drained. "Seven days." He signed off.

Instantly sycophants surrounded him. "All this? To get one cop?" Cairo Fred could not understand.

Some of the best hit men in Europe were at that moment assembled in this very room. "Why don't we take care of it ourselves?," asked Bruce the Knife. It was as though he had been reading Cairo Fred's mind.

"Because"—Dreyfus raised a hand to still the rising clamor—"you wouldn't stand a chance against Clouseau." Raucous laughter and muttered imprecations greeted his words. "You don't know Clouseau," Dreyfus explained.

"He can't be that good." It was Tournier protesting.

"Good." Dreyfus cackled. "No. Clouseau is not good. He is terrible! The worst! He is unlike any man anywhere ever! You cannot even talk about him the way you talk about other men. And you can thank God that there is only one of him. Compared with a dozen Clouseaus, the Doomsday Machine would be a water pistol! Mark my word . . . it will take all the ingenuity of the Great Powers with all of their trained assassins and all of their sophisticated murder weapons to eliminate Clouseau! And even then, there is the chance they might fail."

Even Hindu Harry was impressed. Clouseau, he conceded, did not sound human.

"Human?" Dreyfus laughed. He was beginning to throw a fit. "That is what I have been trying to tell you! Of course he is not human!"

At this very moment, the object of their attention was emerging from the Bayerischerhof lift. Heinrich Beck, former SS colonel and today a successful florist in Augsburg, watched Clouseau cross the lobby. Clouseau dropped his room key at the reception desk, walked out of the hotel, and hailed a taxi.

Heinrich Beck rose inconspicuously and sauntered after Clouseau. As he crossed the lobby, Beck fondled the SS throw knife concealed under his skirt sleeve. The Assassin came out of the hotel just as a taxi pulled up and deposited its passenger. Clouseau was even then crossing the sidewalk intent on entering the taxi.

Beck reached for his knife. Clouseau stopped in the act of getting into the taxi, his eye on an object on the rear seat. The previous passenger had forgotten his briefcase. Clouseau reached into the back seat and picked up the briefcase. Beck aimed his knife toward a spot between Clouseau's third and fourth ribs. Clouseau turned, the briefcase held before him in both hands. Beck's knife plunged into the briefcase.

The porter thought Beck was a common thief attempting to steal the briefcase and jumped him from behind. Clouseau, unaware of the commotion, got into the taxi. "Oktoberfest, *bitte*," he said in his very best German. "Right, guv," responded the driver, who had spent a good part of the war in a British prisoner-of-war camp.

The taxi sped off. Beck continued to struggle with the porter and the owner of the briefcase, who was an off-duty Munich policeman. The policeman shot Beck dead on the spot, then fainted at the realization he had just killed a war hero.

16

In the White House, lights burned late into the night. The President was in an emergency meeting with his closest advisers. He listened intently to the report being delivered by the Secretary of State. It was anything but hopeful.

"As you know," the Secretary was saying, "we had hoped that no one nation would decide to act independently on a matter of such common concern. We even went so far as to try to call an emergency meeting of the Security Council. In the past few hours I have talked personally to Moscow, Peking, London, and Paris, trying to set up a summit conference. The Russians refuse to go to Peking and the Chinese won't go to Moscow." The Secretary sighed and wondered what had impelled him to devote his life to politics.

"It's more than the matter of submitting to international blackmail," he went on worriedly. "Now it's gotten to the point of who is going to get to the Doomsday Machine first. Nor is that the worst of it. It seems every country wants to get the credit for eliminating Clouseau."

"Sort of like a Killers' Olympiad," opined the President.

"Exactly," agreed his Secretary of State, for once not playing the role of yes man to his Chief.

The Director of the CIA cocked an eyebrow. "I think we all are in agreement that we can't allow an unfriendly power—correction, even a *friendly* power —to get hold of Fassbender's ultimate weapon."

The others seated about the room nodded agreement. The Secretary of State brought up an interesting point. Dreyfus, admittedly a lunatic, could be assumed to look very kindly upon the nation whose agent eliminated Clouseau.

The President demurred, saying he considered that a trifle farfetched.

"If somebody had told me a week ago that the UN Building would disappear and that a certified lunatic would be blackmailing the world in order to get rid of one man . . ." began the Head of the Joint Chiefs.

"You've made your point, Oscar," the President acknowledged. "So, what do we do?"

"Clouseau is in Munich," said the man from the CIA, "attending the Oktoberfest. I ordered one of our top people there yesterday with instructions to take Clouseau on sight." He smiled tightly. "I had hoped we might get a slight jump on the competition." The CIA Director placed a comforting arm around the President and tried his best not to alarm him. "We have just learned that twelve countries have their top assassins either in Munich or on their way there. They're all converging on the Oktoberfest."

"My God," said the Secretary of State with a shudder, "It will be like a shooting gallery."

Munich's annual Oktoberfest has been hailed as everything from a gourmand's delight and a beer drinker's heaven to "good family entertainment." Each fall, millions of the lame, the halt, and the thirsty descend upon Munich from as far away as Katmandu and Persepolis and Dar-es-Salaam. Each day during the week of Oktoberfest, the men and women and children of Europe and the lesser continents swill millions of gallons of beer, gorge themselves on thousands of tons of hams and chickens and fish, consume mountains of pretzels, rolls, and pickles, and exude enough perspiration to float the Great White Fleet.

The dazed and happy visitors to Oktoberfest spend the days and nights wandering among the gigantic beer halls erected by Germany's great breweries. Each hall has its own German band and a seating capacity in the thousands. Among the complex of beer halls, food stands, and carnival rides, teams of brewery horses in heavy silver-embossed harnesses stand hitched to massive brewery wagons outside the individual beer gardens. People dance and sing and cry and throw up and make love and have a wonderful time as they lay aside the twin burdens of responsibility and respectability.

Clouseau mingled with the happy crowd of celebrators thronging the midway, suspecting everyone and no one. He was looking, but for what?

Meanwhile Clouseau himself was being looked at. In particular he was being looked at and followed by an innocuous-looking scholarly Chinese gentleman. Appearances in this case was decidedly deceiving. Lin Huon Liu was Red China's premier killer. So intent was he on Clouseau that the Honorable Mr. Lin was totally unaware that he was himself being stalked by the number-one Egyptian assassin.

Clouseau wandered into a funhouse where European children screamed at painted monsters and pretended to be frightened out of their wits. From behind one of the painted monsters, a Polish agent disguised as a mermaid trained a rifle on Clouseau. The Mermaid found it impossible to get a clear shot at her target because of several nuns and their youthful charges who continually got in the way.

Clouseau drifted back onto the midway. By the Mathaser bierstadt, pausing to admire the fine harness on the brewery Percherons, he stepped into a pile of purest Percheron manure. As Clouseau leaned down to wipe his shoe, the Mermaid fired from the funhouse, missing him and drilling through the heart a Nigerian assassin lying in wait for Clouseau under the brewery wagon.

Clouseau shook an admonishing finger at the dead Nigerian, whom he considered to be just another Oktoberfest lush. Then he hauled him to his feet and propped him against the Honorable Mr. Lin. "Keep an eye on him, there's a good fellow," Clouseau murmured and lost himself in the ground as the Egyptian assassin stepped squarely in the way of Lin's silencer-equipped pistol. The handgun spoke and the Egyptian sat down, quite dead.

The Cuban assassin, disguised as a Pretzel Seller, swaggered up to Clouseau and offered a poisoned pretzel. Clouseau politely accepted it and handed it to a Belgian beauty who was known in the underworld as Brussels Betty. Betty bit and died on the spot as Clouseau, totally unaware of the trail of the dead and dying being left in his wake, strolled under the roof for a closer look at the excellent and enthusiastic Mathaser bierstadt musicians.

The Italian assassin, a midget dressed as a Little Boy in American Indian dress, stalked Clouseau down the aisle, drawing his bow. A Brünnhilde of a waitress with an enormous bosom, the Norwegian Killer, bumped Clouseau with a tray heaped with sausages and one-liters of beer. Gallantly Clouseau helped to steady the tray that the waitress deposited on a table before a family from Uber Pfaffenhofen. The waitress flung her brawny arms about Clouseau in a seeming gesture of gratitude, and endeavored to impale him on twin daggers concealed in her brass-studded jerkin.

The Italian assassin saw what was intended and neatly tripped the waitress, who fell on her own daggers and died for the glory of Norway. Clouseau turned and patted the adorable Little Boy in American Indian dress on the head. On the bandstand, the flutist (a hired killer from Rhodesia doubling in the reed section) bent over his music stand and furtively blew a poisoned dart at Clouseau. The poisoned dart struck home in the Hungarian Lingerie Salesman who was trying to get at Clouseau with a strangler's loop of piano wire.

The father of the family from Uber Pfaffenhofen, who knew nothing about assassins or political assassination, picked up the Italian Little Boy and plumped him down on his knee. "Look, Mama," the German father nudged his frau. "Such a cute liddle boy."

76

"Put me down, you big shit," screamed the Italian and raised his tomahawk.

"Oooh, Papa!" The Hausfrau entered into the game, feigning terror. "He is going to scalp us!"

On the bandstand the flutist reached for his second poisoned dart and vowed not to miss again. Clouseau saw the beautiful Italian Little Boy struggling with someone who looked like Nazism personified. Clouseau pulled the Little Boy away from the German father. As Clouseau turned to rebuke the man from Uber Pfaffenhofen, the Italian midget tried to plunge a steel-tipped arrow into Clouseau's jugular.

"See here," lumbered the German father. "Who the hell do you think you are?" Being German, he pronounced the work "tink."

"I am Chief Inspector Clouseau of the French Sûreté and if you lay a finger on this adorable Little Boy I will have you arrested as a child molester." Clouseau reached for his identification as the flutist blew another flat note, his dart striking the midget in the neck under his golden locks, where it could not be seen. The midget expired in Clouseau's arms.

"Now see what you have done," Clouseau reprimanded. "The poor child is exhausted. I wonder where his parents are?" Clouseau looked about just as a legitimate waitress came by. "I suggest you take this cute Little Boy to the children's lost-and-found department." Clouseau handed the child to her.

He turned to the German father with a final word of admonition. "Drink your beer and stop picking on children half your size," he warned, "or I shall see to it that you are prosecuted to the fullest extend of the law."

The German glared at Clouseau. "Your face resembles a baboon's ass," he said threateningly.

"I accept your apology." Clouseau bowed. "Only, do not let it happen again."

Clouseau moved down the aisle to the men's room. At a table across the huge hall the Mexican assassin got up and went after Clouseau just as an East German killer followed him.

By a miracle, the stinking public toilet was nearly deserted. Clouseau waited patiently in the small line of sweating ale addicts. When his turn came, he stepped into a cubicle and sat down. The Mexican stepped into the adjoining cubicle and drew his gun. The East German entered the cubicle on the other side of Clouseau's. The two assassins fired into the cubicle between them, their bullets flying harmlessly above Clouseau's head and into the adjoining cubicles. The Mexican's bullet took the shorter East German between the eyes. The East German's bullet hit the Mexican squarely on the third button of his fringed bolero jacket. The two killers died instantly.

In his cubicle, Clouseau stood up and flushed. He emerged from the toilet and washed his hands. "Nothing is happening here," Clouseau said to his likeness in the mirror. "I might as well go back to the hotel and get a good night's sleep."

17

At precisely 4:54 A.M. on a wet and drizzling Thursday in Washington, D.C., a coded message was received at CIA headquarters. The message was datelined "Munich" and labeled "Urgent." When he was done, the decoding agent triple-checked his work for accuracy. Cursing, he reached for his telephone and called the director of the department just as he was going to bed.

The director listened attentively, commended the agent on his initiative, and then placed a call to the White House, where he asked for the President.

The switchboard operator at 1600 Pennsylvania Avenue protested. "Have you any idea what time it is?"

"The President is waiting for this call," the director

assured. "Now please put me through. Unless you would like to have your income tax returns audited."

As so happened in moments of grave national crisis, the Chief Executive was on his back, asleep, snoring heavily. The First Lady lifted the receiver, listened, and then began to shake her husband. The President sat up groggily. "I'll veto the damn bill" were his first words, before he was fully awake. He stared at the telephone his wife held out to him. "Who is it at this ungodly hour?"

The First Lady shrugged. Who always was it at this ungodly hour? It was, she decided, the story of her marriage: unwanted phone calls at ungodly hours. For the briefest of moments she yearned for her days as a teenage high-school cheerleader in South Turkey Creek, North Carolina.

The cursing of her husband brought her out of the reverie. The President, pale and shaking, listened to the report that detailed the deaths in Munich, within a matter of hours, of nine of the world's most dangerous and heretofore successful professional killers. Although there was no direct proof of their assassin, in each instance the deaths were being credited to Jacques Clouseau.

"Jesus," groaned the President. Now he understood Dreyfus's preoccupation with having Clouseau eliminated. "How many are left in the ball game? . . . Just two? Who are they? . . . Just our guy and the Russian?" The President let out a small sigh. "At least we made it to the finals."

The American agent assigned to eliminate Clouseau was a strapping former Green Beret who bore a remarkable likeness to Omar Sharif. The agent, code name Big Fella, strolled unnoticed into the Bayerischerhof and pushed the lift button. He got off at the fifth floor, walked quickly to suite 556, and let himself in with a skeleton key.

Suite 556 consisted of a sitting room, bedroom, and bath. The suite was in darkness. Big Fella turned on the lights, made a quick check of the living room and

79

bathroom, and returned to the living room, where he turned out the lights and settled down to wait, unaware that Tournier was parking his 1967 Citroën with the cracked backup light a short distance from the hotel.

Nor did Big Fella have any way of knowing that Tournier was in disguise. The Bank Robber wore a Clouseau-like trench coat and felt hat. Tournier opened the lid of a professional actor's makeup box on the seat beside him. Adjusting the rear-view mirror, Tournier snapped on the overhead light. From the makeup kit he took a Clouseau-like moustache, which he affixed to his upper lip with spirit gum. Tournier examined his likeness in the mirror. "You fool," he tested in a voice that matched Clouseau's perfectly. Satisfied, Tournier relocked the makeup box, got out of the car and headed for the hotel.

The Night Clerk scarcely looked at the man standing at the desk before him. "My key, please," said Tournier, "and be quick about it or I shall be forced to have speaks with your superiors."

Dutifully the clerk passed over the key. "Good night, Inspector," he said and went back to reading *The Rise and Fall of the Third Reich*. With the key to suite 556 in his pocket, Tournier walked slowly across the lobby and into the lift.

The beautiful woman who had been watching him, uncrossed her sensational legs and rose from the settee to follow.

In suite 556 Big Fella stiffened at the sound of a key in the lock. Every instinct told him that this, at last, was his prey, the elusive Clouseau, coming home to certain death. Big Fella waited in the shadows, flexing powerful fingers. The door swung open. Tournier entered in the Clouseau disguise. He was a dead man before he lifted his hand.

Big Fella simply pinched off the flow of blood in Tournier's carotid artery. When his victim was unconscious, he carried him into the bathroom where he broke Tournier's neck. Big Fella took his time going through the dead man's pockets. As he anticipated, he found nothing. Big Fella hid the body in the tub, then drew the shower curtain. While this was going on, the beautiful woman with the sensational legs (actually they were her worst feature) was letting herself into suite 556 with her own, made-in-Moscow passkey. Next Lethal Lena, who was the première killer in all the USSR, walked into the bedroom, took off all her clothes, and climbed into bed.

The moment Big Fella came out of the bathroom into the darkened bedroom he saw Lethal Lena lying seductively against the silken pillows and smiling at him. "Good evening, Inspector," the beautiful woman breathed throatily. Big Fella relaxed his grip on the automatic in his pocket and moved toward the bed. "I couldn't sleep," she apologized. "I just happened to be in the neighborhood." She began licking Big Fella's ear. "I hope you don't mind."

Big Fella shook his head. He realized instantly that the beautiful stranger had mistaken him for Clouseau, for whom she apparently had some sort of sexual hunger. Big Fella was no fool. If, in the darkened room, he looked like Clouseau he certainly wouldn't sound like Clouseau once he made the mistake of opening his mouth. Big Fella decided to restrict communication on his part to occasional sighs and tender murmurs, to play it cool and see what happened.

It did, very soon. One moment Big Fella was kissing the beautiful woman's arm. Then he was kissing her neck. "Ohhh, Inspector," moaned the lady in Clouseau's bed. Big Fella found her mouth. The sensational legs kicked back the covers and Big Fella prepared to lay down his life for his country.

In the lobby downstairs a night porter was vacuuming the floors. His brother-in-law, an electrician, was atop a tall ladder replacing light bulbs in the huge, crystal chandelier. Clouseau turned in off the street, having walked all the way from the Oktoberfest grounds. There were no taxis and the few taxi drivers around were in no condition to drive.

Clouseau was tired. His feet hurt. He tripped over the cord of the vacuum cleaner and swore. He fell into the ladder and swore again. When the ladder toppled out from under the electrician, it was the electrician who swore even as he grabbed hold of the chandelier to keep from falling. The vacuum in his brother-in-law's hand began spewing dirt all over the lobby.

Up to the desk marched Clouseau. Oblivious of the chaos in his wake, Clouseau held out his hand. "My key," he commanded.

The Night Clerk was growing bored with Clouseau. "But you have your key."

"If I had my key," Clouseau countered with maddening logic, "would I be standing here in the middle of your filthy lobby, asking you for my key? Answer me that, you fool!"

"I gave you your key when you came in half an hour ago." The Night Clerk was beginning to have grave reservations, if not of Clouseau's sanity, then at least of his memory.

"You gave it to me when I came in half an hour ago," Clouseau parroted.

"Yes," replied the poor Night Clerk and he thought about re-enlisting.

Clouseau fixed the man with a chilling eye. "You know who I am." The Night Clerk nodded.

"You are Inspector—"

"*Chief* Inspector," thundered Clouseau. "Remember that, until I am promoted again!"

"You are Chief Inspector Clouseau," the Night Clerk said dully.

"Of the Sûreté," Clouseau prompted.

"Of the Sûreté," echoed the night clerk.

"And do you know how I became Chief Inspector Clouseau of the Sûreté?," asked Chief Inspector Clouseau of the Sûreté.

"No," grumbled the Night Clerk. "But I suppose you will tell me."

Clouseau beamed at his captive audience of one. "I became Chief Inspector Clouseau of the Sûreté by being a first-rate detective. Shall I give you an example of how a first-rate detective operates?"

"Do I have a choice?" bartered the Night Clerk.

Clouseau set his astonishing powers of deduction in

82

operation. "A first-rate detective would instantly deduce that you are German. About thirty-eight years old."

"Thirty-nine," interrupted the Night Clerk, "but I have a young face."

"You are also an alcoholic," Clouseau said accusingly.

"How do you know that?," asked the Night Clerk, who thought he had kept his secret fairly well.

"Because," said a triumphant Clouseau, "a half hour ago you were so drunk you gave someone else my key!"

The Night Clerk struggled to retain the lessons he had learned in Night Clerk School. To hell with tact and courtesy to hotel guests! The Night Clerk leaned on his desk and snarled, "I suggest that it is the first-rate detective who is so drunk he has forgotten that a half hour ago he came in, picked up his key, and went up to his room!"

Clouseau stood his ground. "A first-rate detective would also deduce that if you persist in this infuriating stubbornness you will be fired from your job and you will have no money with which to buy any more of your wretched schnapps."

The Night Clerk knew when he was licked. "In that case," he said humbly, "I have no alternative but to admit my mistake and give you another key." So saying, the poor fellow gave Clouseau the key and, when Clouseau turned his back, the finger as well.

In suite 556 Big Fella slipped out of bed where Lethal Lena lay blissfully asleep. As he started to dress, Big Fella hummed happily to himself, and vowed to have a talk with his superiors on the considerable merits of détente. When he was dressed, Big Fella let himself out the door of the suite just as Clouseau was unlocking the outside bedroom door with the key the stupid Night Clerk had given him. Big Fella walked down the hall, whistling.

Clouseau groped his way from the bedroom into the sitting room. As he went through the door, the beautiful woman awoke and stretched. Lena slipped out of

83

bed and went into the bathroom. Clouseau re-entered the bedroom carrying the copy of the evening paper he had found in the sitting room. He turned to the sports pages and, sitting on the bed, started to undress. Clouseau made a note to have a word with the assistant manager in the morning about the maid who had neglected to make his bed. Clouseau put on his pajamas and went into the sitting room, where he turned out the light he had left on forgetfully. During his absence, the beautiful woman emerged from the bathroom and stopped short in the doorway. Either he was losing his mind or a very beautiful and very undressed lady was sitting bolt upright in his bed, smiling at him in a most seductive manner.

18

"Come back to bed, my darling." The beautiful woman must be speaking to him! Clouseau turned to make sure no one was standing behind him. "Unless, of course, you are too tired." She smiled secretively.

"Tired?" Clouseau found the thought preposterous. "What should make me feel tired? Certainly not an eight-mile walk into town!"

"Truly you are magnificent," cooed the beautiful woman. Clouseau nodded modestly. "Only first take off those ridiculous pajamas."

"Pajamas?" Clouseau wondered what she could possibly mean by that. "Of course," he agreed, playing for time. "But don't you think I should brush my teeth first?"

His beautiful companion made a face. "Hurry," she inplored.

Clouseau trotted across the carpet and into the bathroom, where he pantomimed brushing his teeth and gargling. His mind raced. What to do? From the other room the beautiful woman called out to him. "Please hurry, darling."

Clouseau thought of a cold shower. He pulled back the shower curtain, leaned in to turn on the spray, and stared directly into the sightless eyes of the departed Tournier. At last Clouseau knew precisely what he had to do. He picked up the bathroom phone and dialed room service.

"This is Chief Inspector Clouseau in suite 556. There is a beautiful woman in my bed and a dead man in my bathtub." The bathroom door opened. Lena stood there, Clouseau's trench coat carelessly flung over her shoulders. The coat only accented her nakedness.

"If you are going to take a bath," she said, with her lethal smile, "I want to take one with you."

Clouseau dropped the telephone and raised a shaking hand.

"Madame," he said, "I arrest you for the murder of the man in my bathtub. You have the right to remain silent. You have the right to counsel."

"What?" shouted the beautiful woman. 'Why don't we quit fooling around and start fooling around again? You scrub my back. I'll scrub yours."

Lena turned on the hot-water faucet in the shower. Spray began to fall gently on Tournier's fake Clouseau moustache.

"Who is this fellow?" Clouseau asked. "He looks familiar."

"He looks like you," said his companion and leaned in to turn off the water. Clouseau could see that she had sensational legs as well as other parts that were not too bad, either. First things first, Clouseau decided. The corpse could wait. But what was the foolish beautiful woman doing pulling off the dead man's fake moustache?

"Tournier!" gasped Clouseau, and sat down on the edge of the tub.

The beautiful woman put on the fake moustache and leered at Clouseau. "Tournier!" she mimicked.

"'The Bank Robber," Clouseau responded.

The beautiful woman frowned prettily and perched on the side of the tub beside him. "What is he doing in your bathtub dressed like you?"

"I might ask you the same question," Clouseau said with startling lucidity.

"His neck has been broken. I am not that strong. Believe me." Lena caressed Clouseau. She put her arms about his neck and took off a large ruby ring. "It was to be for you," she confessed. She pressed the underside of the ring, showing Clouseau the tiny, poison needle concealed in the shank.

Clouseau smiled. "Thank you, but I am not in the habit of wearing jewelry."

"You do not understand," Lena said, breathing huskily into his ear. The little hairs along Clouseau's neck goose-stepped in unison. "I am Lena Berriossiva, Lethal Lena, of the NKVD. Until an hour ago, when you taught me the true meaning of patriotism in there"—she nodded toward the rumpled bed—"I was a loyal Soviet agent under orders from the Presidium to kill you."

Clouseau stared uncomprehendingly from Tournier to Lena.

"I was considered the perfect liquidator," Lena Berriossiva sobbed. "Because no man has ever been able to involve me emotionally . . . until tonight. Do you think you could fall in love with an ex-Russian agent with a moustache?" she asked adorably.

Clouseau pondered. "I suppose it is possible," he agreed, "provided you were to remove your ring."

Lena quickly stripped the murder weapon from her finger. She looked at the needle. "Just one little prick," she mused. "And I might never have known." Lena kissed Clouseau passionately. He kissed her in return. Lena pushed him away. Something was not the same. This was not the same man who had made beautiful love to her in the other room not twenty minutes before! Something was terribly wrong! "You've changed!" Lena cried. "The sparkle in your eye has gone!"

"Well," Clouseau remarked philosophically, "I suppose a dead man in the bathtub could make a difference."

Clouseau began pacing back and forth in the bathroom, no small feat, since the room was anything but spacious. "I suspect that poor Tournier can lead me to the man that it is my sworn duty to apprehend."

Lena stood up and began to take off Clouseau's trench coat with the nothing-on-underneath-it. "I, too, had a sworn duty but I have forsaken it, become a traitor, given up everything . . . for you!" Lena allowed the coat to slip to the floor.

"I can appreciate your problem," Clouseau sympathized. "And I wish I could help you."

"Please," begged Lena. "Just one more hour."

"Believe me, it would be my pleasure," the gallant detective said.

"Mine, too," said Lena, with a chuckle.

"With me, it is duty first." Clouseau jumped to his feet and clicked his heels.

"Just this once,'" pleaded Lena, "make an exception."

"Farewell, my lovely," Clouseau sighed. He kissed Lena tenderly and started to leave the room. Something drew him back. Poor Tournier, Clouseau thought. He would look so much better with his hands folded. Clouseau lifted the dead man's hand and saw for the first time the tattoo of an ancient crest in the center of the palm.

"Odd," Clouseau ruminated. "Tournier did not have this funny little tattoo a month ago when I had the pleasure of sending him to prison for life."

Lena glanced at the tattoo. "It looks like the Mondschein crest."

Clouseau had never heard of the Mondscheins. "I think we studied about them when I was in the eighth grade," said Lena, trying to recall her junior-high-school history. "Weren't they an ancient and infamous family that ruled Bavaria in the fifteenth century? I think I read somewhere that Mondschein castle, the family seat, had been sold recently."

At the word castle Clouseau bolted into the other room and began throwing his clothes on. Lena wandered in and sat on the bed, watching him. "Somehow, I got the impression you were a bigger man," she vouchsafed.

"Yes, I have been known to give that impression." Clouseau zipped up his fly, nearly tearing the nail off his thumb.

"But then, from another angle, your shoulders are quite broad. Your chest is rather deep and hairy," Lena mused.

"That is because I take after my mother's side of the family," Clouseau explained.

"Your father was a very lucky man." Lena smiled somewhat lewdly.

"My maternal grandmother had the face of an angel and the build of a stevedore," Clouseau recalled fondly. "Everybody called her Marlon."

Clouseau sat on the bed and began putting on his shoes, double-tying the laces as he had been taught in school.

"You think you will find your man in Mondschein Castle?" Lena began to disconcert Clouseau by tickling him under the chin with her bare foot.

Clouseau tried to concentrate on police work. "I am sure of it."

"I don't suppose it coul wait." Lena's soft little heel rubbed Clouseau's left eyelid.

"He is a madman and a kidnapper—and I adore your precious little feet," announced Clouseau. The telephone on the night table began ringing. With his last ounce of self-control Clouseau picked up the hated instrument. "Yes?" he shouted in a fury. It was the house detective on the other end. Clouseau was on the point of inviting the man to go to hell.

"You reported a beautiful woman in your bed and a dead man in your bathtub," said the house detective, Gunther Kojak. "I am on my way up to investigate."

Clouseau's mind raced. 'Somebody is pulling your leg," he announced.

The house detective was insistent—according to the

switchboard operator who had taken the call, it had definitely come from suite 556.

"Then I am afraid somebody is pulling *my* leg," Clouseau replied.

"Are you certain there is no one in your room?" the detective persisted.

"Nor in my bathtub, dead or alive," Clouseau snapped. "I swear it on my grandmother's cargo hook!" Clouseau slammed down the telephone. His eye drifted to the bed, where Lena lay, her naked body luminous in the semidarkness. Clouseau gazed at her lovingly. "There are times when duty can be a royal pain in the derrière," he declared.

"Will I see you again?" cried Lena.

"Unless I am killed in the line of duty or in some other way," promised Clouseau.

"Kiss me good-bye." Lena rose from the bed like some Botticellian vision.

"I cannot," Clouseau said wretchedly. "Because there are times when a man is likely to say to hell with duty and the fatherland, and I cannot afford to let this be one of those times." Clouseau marched bravely out of the bedroom and into the sitting room, where he fell over the desk, picked himself up, and limped out into the hall. As she shut the door, Lena picked up the telephone and dialed a local number.

"French Embassy? I would like to make an appointment to come down and defect."

19

Former Chief Inspector Dreyfus beamed at the breakfast laid out before him. Prunes. Bran muffins. Yogurt. Orange juice. Three four-minute eggs. This was going to be a glorious day. Dreyfus felt it in his bones. A magnificent day. On this, the sixth day since his ultimatum to the world, either. Clouseau would die or Dreyfus would unleash the awesome power of the Doomsday Machine once again and wipe out Pittsburgh.

Dreyfus lifted his chilled glass of freshly squeezed orange juice and toasted Dr. Fassbender, who sat across the table from him, staring dully into a bowl of gruel.

"Your health." Dreyfus drank and winced. A little wriggling pain flickered in a bicuspid. He must be getting a cavity. No matter. It still remained a glorious day. There would be plenty of time to go to the dentist after Clouseau's funeral. Dreyfus could not wait to see the flag-draped casket, hear the rifle volley from the guard of honor, see Clouseau's hated remains disappear into a hole in the ground. Dreyfus stirred from his reverie. His eggs were growing cold, and the gaunt scientist seemed to be addressing him.

"I have done everything you asked." Fassbender spoke even more softly than usual, his spirit having broken under Dreyfus's ruthless will.

"You have been most co-operative," Dreyfus said generously. "A model prisoner."

"When will Margo and I be permitted to leave here?"

Dreyfus had anticipated the question. "Soon," he lied. "Any day now."

Fassbender read the deception in his captor's words. He knew that he never would walk out of Mondschein Castle. "What you really mean is, you have no intention of letting us go." Fassbender thought of Margo and very nearly broke down. "You intend to continue your reign of terror whether Clouseau is eliminated or not."

Dreyfus toyed with an egg yolk. "I'll admit the thought has occurred to me."

"You're mad," Fassbender choked.

It was not exactly an original thought. Eminent French psychiatrists had pronounced a similar verdict months before, when Dreyfus had not even begun to approach his present condition of advanced schizophrenia.

"And you are redundant, Professor," said Dreyfus smiling. There was nothing quite so agreeable as stimulating tabletalk, he thought. "Redundant and fallacious. Madness does not preclude achievement. You have only to look at Hitler. Or Amin."

Fassbender passed a trembling hand over his brow. Since coming to Mondschein Castle, he suffered constantly from headaches. It must be the foehn, he thought absently. Then he realized that the foehn of his youth blew in Switzerland . . . beautiful, blessed, chocolate-suffused Switzerland on the far side of the Alps. Professor Fassbender realized he was beginning to crack up. He fought for some semblance of sanity.

"At least you cannot operate the Doomsday Machine without me." Would that he had never become a scientist and had remained in his father's dry-goods business! He and Margo would not be in the present, perilous situation.

Dreyfus smiled. "Until you have taught me." The toothache was becoming an irritant . . . a nuisance.

"And if I refuse to teach you?" Fassbender nearly scored a point for the good guys.

"Then, regrettably, I will be forced to take up the matter with your daughter." The villainous Dreyfus bit angrily into a bran muffin.

Fassbender slumped in his chair, his deep-set eyes burning with an unholy light. "What kind of a man are you?"

"A madman!" boasted Dreyfus. "You said so yourself!"

Cairo Fred rushed into the room brandishing a cablegram: CLOUSEAU MATTER CONCLUDED AS PER INSTRUCTIONS STOP CHALK ONE UP FOR THE GOOD OLD USA. It was signed BIG FELLA.

Dreyfus exploded out of his seat. Raising his arms, he began a wild, capering dance about the room. And as he danced, he sang in a cracked, exulting tremolo:

"Round and round the grave we dance,
Clouseau won't be back in France,
Jacques is dead and laid to rest,
A weight's been lifted from my chest!"

"Not bad, boss," acknowledged Cairo Fred, who owned some books of poetry.

Abruptly Dreyfus stopped whirling. He seized Cairo Fred by the lapels and spoke directly into his face. "Tell me how he died! I want to know where and when! Spare not a single detail."

Cairo Fred pulled away. "Early this morning," he wheezed. "In his hotel room. Of a broken neck. The maid found his body in the bathtub."

"Are you sure?" Dreyfus savored the moment of triumph.

"Would an American agent lie?" retorted Cairo Fred. "I mean, if you can't believe in the CIA, what's left to believe in?" He pushed a box toward Dreyfus. "Have a chocolate."

Dreyfus bit into a cherry cream, and shrieked in agony as the sweet hit the cavity. The noise woke Hindu Harry, who was asleep three floors below in the Hessian Suite. Hindu Harry shot up the stairs three steps at a time to the side of his stricken leader. Dreyfus had both hands in his mouth. His eyes were rolling like tuna clippers caught in a hurricane.

"Ook a' i'." Dreyfus pointed into his mouth. Hindu Harry looked at Cairo Fred in confusion. Cairo Fred did not have the slightest idea what Dreyfus wanted. Fassbender could have explained, of course, but Fassbender found himself rather enjoying Dreyfus's anguish.

Dreyfus rushed to a desk and, dashing off a note, held it under Hindu Harry's nose. "Look in my mouth, you asshole," Hindu Harry dutifully read. "I think I have a cavity."

Hindu Harry moved to comply. "Gee, Boss," he queried, "why didn't you say so?" He pulled Dreyfus's stubby little fingers away from the offending bicuspid and quickly located a small black spot just at the gumline. "It looks like a cavity, all right," Hindu Harry said cheerfully. "A bad one. You need a dentist."

"You know perfectly well I can't allow any outsider in this castle." With his fingers out of his mouth Dreyfus was able to speak more intelligibly.

Professor Fassbender delivered a weighty scientific opinion. "Then you will just have to suffer."

"Screw you!" shouted Dreyfus. He poured himself a tremendous shot of brandy. "This is my day of rejoicing! Clouseau is dead and I should be in a state of grace!"

Dreyfus swallowed the brandy and felt a little better. Something, however, kept nagging at him, as though trying to spoil his fun. He turned to Cairo Fred once again.

"Now hear this!" Dreyfus raised his voice. "I want one-hundred-percent verification. Eyewitness identification, if possible! Go to Munich. Poke around. Talk to the hotel maid who found the body. I have a terrible feeling, call it a foreboding, that all is not so good. Bring me proof. Absolute proof. For only then can I be happy!"

Cairo Fred hurried from the room as Dreyfus lifted the brandy bottle.

Far below in the valley, Clouseau drove his rented Fiat up a winding, one-track dirt road, and into the front yard of the tiny Hotel Alpenros. He got out, neglecting to set the hand brake. The Fiat rolled backward across the lawn, flattening two croquet wickets, a small outcropping of edelweiss, and a goose before coming to rest against a butter churn.

Clouseau entered the Alpenros. An ancient clerk in lederhosen sat behind the desk, picking his false teeth. A huge Alsatian dog lay at his feet. *"Guten Tag."* Clouseau spoke flawless German.

"Good day," said the clerk, popping his teeth back into his mouth. "Can I be of service?"

"Maybe yes, maybe no." Clouseau slipped into his new role. "I am Professor Guy Gadbois, Medieval

Castle Authority from Marseille. I understand the Mondschein Castle is not far from where we stand. I would like to have a look at it—for my castle research, you understand."

The clerk made a sign indicating that what Clouseau was suggesting was a no-no. "I wouldn't advise it."

"And why not?" Clouseau was very much on the scent now, nostrils twitching, every sense on the qui vive.

"People in the village talk of strange things going on up there at Mondschein Castle." The clerk crossed himself, which was in itself strange, since he was an atheist. "There are signs all over the place, put up by the new owner."

"What sort of signs?" Clouseau had to know.

"Trespassers will be shot," the oldster responded in an offhand manner. "Stuff like that." Clouseau found the man to be utterly charming. So much so, that he made one of the instinctive, on-the-spot decisions for which he was famous.

"Do you have a reum?" He smiled engagingly. The clerk shook his head. "But this is a hotel," Clouseau persisted. This time the clerk nodded. "And it is out of season." Clouseau clearly had the upper hand now.

"That is true," the ancient one agreed.

Clouseau gave away his little secret. "I do not see any guests."

"That is because the last guest left yesterday." The clerk's foot was beginning to go to sleep.

"Then please explain to me why you do not have a reum!" Clouseau shouted.

"Because I do not know what a reum is." The clerk was becoming difficult.

"Ein Zimmer!" Clouseau found the word in a German dictionary that happened to be resting on the desk.

"A room!" The clerk's eyes widened with sudden understanding.

"That is what I have been saying, you idiot." Clouseau scrawled his name across the register. Then he carefully scratched it out and painstakingly wrote in "Guy Gadbois."

As the clerk reached behind him for a key, Clouseau looked admiringly at the Alsatian, who sat licking one forepaw. "Does your dog bite," Clouseau asked idly.

"No." The clerk tossed Clouseau his key. Clouseau bent to pet the animal.

"Nice doggy." The Alsation bared its fangs and lunged at Clouseau's hand. Clouseau hurriedly snatched it back. "I thought you said that your dog does not bite," he remonstrated.

The clerk looked levelly at Clouseau. "But," he said, "that is not my dog."

20

The First Lady was a country girl at heart. She stood now in the White House kitchen, scrambling eggs for her husband. The First Lady loved these very occasional moments they were able to share, when the household staff had gone off to bed and the various aides and departmental heads had scattered to their homes in Virginia. The First Lady loved to cook, even though the food she served was not fit to eat. But because he loved her, the President gamely swallowed the meals his spouse placed before him with such pride. It was the opinion of the President's physician that home cooking was slowly but surely shortening his famous patient's life.

The First Lady, the former Ella Mae Sparrow of South Turkey Creek, North Carolina, worried about her husband. Much as she tried to hide the fact from him, she knew in her heart that he knew she worried about him, and this had the effect of making her even more worried. Washington gossip columnists referred to the President and the First Lady as the capital's most devoted couple. It was common knowledge they shared the same Valium bottle.

"Sunnyside up, hon." The First Lady spooned the greasy mess onto her husband's plate. "Just the way you like them."

The Chief Executive picked up his fork dutifully. "You don't understand, Ella Mae. Sunnyside up is for fried eggs. These are scrambled . . . I think." He put his fork aside. His wife came over and sat in his lap, which was something he disliked almost as much as her cooking. "You look worried." She hazarded a wild guess: "You don't like your breakfast."

The White House kitchen clock showed 2:45 A.M.

"It's not that," the President admitted with rare candor. "It's this damned Clouseau affair."

The First Lady could not understand. "I thought Chuck nailed the bastard last night in his hotel room in Munich," she replied. The President winced.

"Not 'Chuck,'" he cautioned. The President looked around the room. "This place may be bugged. If you have to talk about Chuck, use his code name."

"Okay," said the First Lady brightly. "What is his code name?"

"Big Fella," the President reminded her. "You thought it up yourself. Don't you remember?" The First Lady nodded. The President was so preoccupied with the weighty affairs of his office that he failed to notice his lap was beginning to go to sleep. According to the best medical minds, it was an affliction that affected most presidents but very few dictators.

"Don't say anything to your hairdresser," the President warned, "but there seems to be some question whether the man Big Fella took out last night [the President loved to watch cops-and-robbers TV shows], really was Clouseau. I have asked the Sûreté to send us his fingerprints for comparison with those of the dead man."

The First Lady counted the gray hairs on her husband's head. There were so many now. "Claude told me he heard that that awful Lena what's-her-name has defected to the French." Claude, the First Lady's hairdresser, had a direct line into the White House. "Claude says the Kremlin's so mad they could spit." The President chuckled at the good news. "Claude also said he heard, unofficially, of course, that Clouseau had been spotted in the woods around Mondschein Castle." The President stopped chuckling. "You're going to send a special task force to investigate, aren't you?" asked the First Lady. The President nodded. He reached for the phone that was tied in directly to the Pentagon.

"You can damn well bet your scrambled eggs we're not going to be the only ones checking it out," he grumbled.

"If that's where the Doomsday Machine is," remarked the First Lady, "let's just pray that our boys get there first."

Clouseau hurried through the Gruppenwald, coiling his rope. He was outfitted as an Alpine mountain climber in lederhosen, woolen knee socks that made his calves itch, heavy climbing boots equipped with crampons, and leather gloves. He carried a short-handled pick and a well-thumbed copy of *Dent's Mountaineering*.

As he trotted through the Gruppenwald, a dense forest known for its heavy growth of thicket, Clouseau kept an eye out for wild boars. The big tuskers were a particular nuisance during this, the mating season.

Clouseau consulted the map he had drawn of the area surrounding Mondschein Castle. It showed the location of electrified fences as well as the mine-seeded turnip fields along the southern slopes. Clouseau continued to push in a northerly direction. It was two hours since he had left the Hotel Alpenros. In that time he had covered exactly half a mile.

He was panting heavily as he stepped from a clearing and gazed at last at the grim gray granite walls of Mondschein. They towered forty feet above him and there was not so much as a sparrow's foothold to be seen in the closely joined stones. Indeed, the only access to the castle was by a drawbridge spanning not a conventional moat, but a raging mountain torrent that would have put the Colorado rapids to shame.

Clouseau stood on the shore, trying to make up his mind. He received unexpected help. A wild boar with an enormous erection trotted out of a dense glade and surveyed Clouseau with a mixture of curiosity and lust. *"Sus scrofa!"* In his panic Clouseau used the zoological name for the beast. Thank God the grappling hook had already been attached to his climbing rope!

Clouseau quickly paid out some twenty feet of line, swung it around his head, and let fly. The hook sailed unerringly toward the topmost timbers of the drawbridge, where it snagged securely. Clouseau waded into the stream, his teeth chattering in the forty-degree water. He fought the current, bare knees turning blue, and, inch-by-inch, made his way to the bridge, literally pulling himself hand over hand.

Not until then did Clouseau take note of the fact that the drawbridge was in the up position on the castle side of the river. Clouseau worked in the bone-chilling water to free his line. It took him twenty-five minutes and by the time he had the grappling hook in his hand, he was exhausted. He looked from Mondschein Castle to the bank behind him, where the love-starved boar still stood his ground. New strength flowed into Clouseau's arms and legs. Once again he coiled his rope, swung it around his head, and threw. This time the grappling hook caught the underside of the drawbridge, halfway up, burying itself in the soft pine planking.

Clouseau began to pull himself up the rope and out of the water. Once free of the current, he found himself able to move faster. He was little more than half-way up to the hook when he was alerted by the sound of someone starting a car in the castle courtyard. The drawbridge began to come down. Clouseau climbed faster but the faster he went, the more ground he lost to the descending drawbridge, which banged down, plunging him into the water. Then a car drove over the bridge from inside Mondschein Castle and, once across, turned onto the valley road. The drawbridge was pulled up again. Clouseau hung doggedly to his rope for a moment but then lost his grip, toppled into the water, and was swept away. The boar, watching Clouseau floating downriver, seemed rather saddened by the spectacle.

Comrade Rosmenko was in Lubyanka Prison interviewing a onetime job applicant (the job for which the unfortunate man had applied was Rosmenko's own), when the call from Munich was put through. The First Secretary of the Politburo listened with a sense of growing excitement. The Americans had failed! The dead man had been identified as an unimportant French bank robber named Tournier. Despite the defection of the traitorous Lena Berriossiva, the Soviet Union was still in the ball game!

Rosmenko barked orders. A Special Force of limited striking power, armed with nuclear weapons, was to be sent forthwith to Mondschein Castle from a secret base on the East German border.

"They should arrive in a couple of hours," Rosmenko reported to the Party Leader.

"And the Americans?" asked the Party Leader. It was a question Rosmenko dreaded.

"Already on the way," he admitted. "Also the English, the French, the Dutch . . . everyone. Even Uganda. It will be a close race."

The Party Leader cursed in his native Georgian, a sure sign that he was deeply troubled. "It is a race, Comrade Rosmenko, that we cannot afford to lose," he said.

At Mondschein Castle the drawbridge was up. Small icicles formed on the underside of its rough planking. A car drove up on the woods side of the river and sounded its horn three times. The drawbridge was lowered. From the woods behind the car Clouseau emerged, running low. As the car started across the drawbridge, Clouseau scrambled onto the rear bumper and hung on. The car drove over the bridge and into the castle courtyard. Clouseau dropped off and hid in a culvert. From his place of concealment he watched as Cairo Fred got out of the car. Hindu Harry met him on the steps leading to Mondschein Castle. The drawbridge was pulled up, cutting off Clouseau's only escape.

Clouseau found some measure of consolation in his present predicament. At least he had gotten into Mondschein Castle and away from the love-maddened boar.

He looked around as Cairo Fred and Hindu Harry, still talking earnestly, entered the castle. There was a heavy grate in the wall beside Clouseau. He removed it with difficulty. The grate covered some sort of opening. Clouseau climbed into the opening and commenced crawling along the inside of what appeared to be some long-unused drainage pipe. The way was easier now. Up ahead Clouseau thought he saw light. He stopped to light a match. A sudden gust of air blew out the match. The faint sound of rushing water came to his ears. The sound grew louder until it became a roar. A column of water caught Clouseau before he could move, and swept him down past the opening through which he had climbed, and deep into the drainage system below the castle.

Clouseau was carried along in the dark, bobbing and swirling and ducking in the tide. He had no idea where he was. As Clouseau fought to stay afloat, he thought of the sewers of his beloved Paris. Then, astonishingly, he was swept out into strong sunlight through the outfall hole in the castle wall. Clouseau found himself falling once again into the icy river and being swept downstream.

Upstairs in Mondschein Castle, Dreyfus tried to keep his mind off his raging toothache by playing the giant Wurlitzer. He played "Rudolf the Red-nosed Reindeer," "Happy Talk," "Swingin' on a Star"—every happy tune he could think of. Nothing seemed to help.

Dreyfus stopped midway through a chorus of "Take Me Out to the Ball Game."

"I can't stand it any more!" he screamed at Hindu Harry. "You better send for a dentist."

Even as Hindu Harry ran for the car, a canoe from upstream swept down on the castle. Clouseau stood upright in the canoe. The drawbridge was lowered as the unseen canoe swept downstream toward it. The car drove over the drawbridge, its occupants unaware of Clouseau, who reached for the support timbers of the drawbridge and regretted not being six feet tall. Clouseau's stretching fingers missed the drawbridge by inches. He was swept downstream once again, his mind working frantically on a new scheme to storm the walls of Mondschein Castle.

In the upper meadows of the Wispile, far above the castle, members of the Bavarian Hang Gliders Club were holding their semiannual love-in and soaring competition. The thoroughly sodden Clouseau moved cautiously among the rutting couples, until he came across an exhausted honeymoon pair who were only too happy to rent their hang glider with the red-and-black sails to the persuasive Frenchman.

As they helped Clouseau into the harness, they tried to explain the mysteries of updrafts and downdrafts and swirling mountain air currents. Clouseau nodded and allowed himself to be guided to the top of a rather precipitous slope. "Off you go!" shouted the husband gaily. He gave Clouseau a shove. "Happy landings, poopsie!" the bride called after Clouseau as his stubby little legs carried him down the hillside. Faster and faster ran Clouseau. Then, suddenly, he was airborne! It was fantastic! Clouseau floated on a column of warm air. High above Mondschein Castle, he soared and dipped. He shifted his weight slightly on the control bar and the hang glider responded. Half a mile away the turrets of Mondschein Castle sparkled in the sunlight. Clouseau went into a long, slow glide.

As he neared the castle, his speed increased. Clouseau glided toward a slender turret. His heart leaped as he saw that some careless person had left the window in the turret open. Clouseau let go of the hand glider and prepared to swing in through the open window just as Helga, the upstairs maid, finished dusting the sill and closed the window.

Clouseau crashed through the window into the tiny, circular room. His speed was such that he sailed across the room and out the window on the far side, to fall once again into the mountain torrent he was coming to know so well.

A crescent moon rose over the Gruppenwald, where a boar grunted and slashed at young trees in frustration. On the upper meadows, the happy hang gliders had long since departed.

Clouseau sat in the lobby of the Alpenros, wrapped in a blanket, his feet soaking in a wooden tub of hot water. He was sipping a schnapps.

"You got to be some stubborn nut," the clerk sympathized. He scratched the huge Alsatian back of its jowls. The dog rumbled his gratitude. The phone rang. The clerk made no move to get up. Clouseau half stood up in the bucket.

"Would you mind?" he asked. "I am expecting a telephone call."

Reluctantly, the clerk heaved himself out of his chair and picked up the phone. He listened briefly, nodded, and made vague signs with his hands, which naturally were lost on the caller. "Not in!" the clerk shouted and hung up the telephone. "He's not here and there is no use asking me to take a message." The clerk suddenly realized he had already hung up the phone. He felt foolish. "It was for Dr. Shurz," he explained, "the village dentist. He's gone fishing."

The clerk resumed his seat. "He made my dentures for me. They fit pretty good, too. Unless I try to eat something tough, like schnitzel."

Clouseau's mind was racing. Did he dare ask? "Who was calling Dr. Shurz? That is, if it is not giving away professional secrets." Clouseau smiled.

The clerk explained that somebody at the castle had a toothache. Clouseau leaped from the wooden tub, splashing hot water on the lobby floor and on the Alsatian. The dog howled and ran under a table, upsetting it. "Now see what you have done, you

Medieval Castle Authority, you!" shouted the clerk.

Clouseau fixed the man with a steely glance. "I am not Guy Gadbois, Medieval Castle Authority from Marseille," he admitted. "I am, with all due modesty, the famous Chief Inspector Clouseau of the French Sûreté!" The clerk stared in open-mouthed wonder at his hotel guest. "Quickly," Clouseau snapped. "Show me this *Zimmer!*"

"His what?" Was the man a nitwit?

"His reum!" screamed Clouseau.

"Well why didn't you say so?" The clerk got his passkey. He stopped as a thought suddenly occurred to him. "This is official police business, isn't it?" he asked.

"Top secret," Clouseau barked. The Alsatian lifted his head and howled at the moon. "If you co-operate, there might be a citation in it for you."

The clerk led the way to the room of Dr. Shurz. "If it's all the same," he commented, "I'd rather have the reward money."

Clouseau thought the clerk a greedy swine, although he did not say so openly, for he needed his co-operation. He followed the clerk into Dr. Shurz's room under the eaves. The doctor's little black bag stood on the dresser. Clouseau smiled.

In the valley below, a wood-burning locomotive pulling two passenger coaches and a freight car loaded with cheeses arrived at the depot in Sweissemann, the nearest village on the rail line linking the Alpenros with the outside world.

Four men dressed in blue suits—the Russian Special Force—got off the first coach. Rosmenko himself had given the highly secret undertaking its code word: "Operation Pudding." Once the Soviets had the Doomsday Machine, Rosmenko confided to asssociates, they would have the capacity to make "pudding" of America's SAC bases.

"And," he had boasted, "who knows? We might turn Fort Knox into a nice, crisp biscuit."

The four Russians quickly marched in inconspicuous lock step to the only taxi stand in Sweissemann and climbed into the horse-drawn carriage.

As they were driven off, four men dressed in blue jeans and tank tops—the United States Special Task Force—got off the second coach. Realizing the Russians had played into the trap set for them, that of being first on the scene and into the only buggy, the Americans dashed across the street and into the Hertz car-rental office.

At the door they stopped short. Four Japanese agents disguised as tourists were signing up for the agency's lone vehicle, a 1943 Dodge runabout.

"Quick!" the leader of the United States attack team led his men outside. "We'll hit the Avis office!" As they rushed to the Hertz competitor, a helicopter flew overhead; it was carrying the Swedish team. The Avis office door was locked. Nothing daunted, the resourceful Americans simply crossed the street to the schoolyard, "borrowed" four bicycles, and began pedaling out of town toward Mondschein Castle.

The reason for the unusual closing of the Avis office now became clear. Chief Inspector Clouseau, disguised as the absent Dr. Shurz, drove his rental Avis Edsel up to the riverbank across from the castle and sounded his horn loudly three times. A ragged bumper sticker, "We try harder," fluttered from the Edsel's windshield. Clouseau got out of the Edsel and held up his black doctor's bag in full view of the castle. Cairo Fred, squinting through binoculars at the strange vehicle across the stream, ordered the drawbridge to be lowered. Clouseau climbed back into his car and looked at his image in the rear-view mirror. He made a slight adjustment in the thrust of his fake, wax jaw, kicked the Balls Boutique box under the seat, and drove across the drawbridge at high speed.

Clouseau skidded to a stop in the castle courtyard as Cairo Fred approached the car. Even had Cairo Fred met Jacques Clouseau before, it is doubtful he would have recognized the French detective. Clouseau wore a henna-dyed wig, thick glasses, and a false, wax nose and wax chin.

"I am Dr. Shurz," Clouseau said amiably. "Show me where it hurts."

Cairo Fred gestured toward the massive portcullis guarding the castle entrance. "The patient is in there."

Clouseau bowed his best dentist's bow and hurried into the dreaded fastness of Mondschein Castle. Behind him he heard the sound of the drawbridge being raised once again into its defensive position.

In the doorway he turned for a last look. Some idiot in a helicopter seemed to be doing his best to buzz the castle. And, although he could not be certain, Clouseau thought he caught a glimpse of five parachutists bailing out of a low-flying twin-engine plane before it disappeared behind a hill. Undetectedly by the others, the English parachutists floated to earth.

21

Dreyfus sat in a chair while the doctor unpacked his medical kit. Clouseau knew down to the last detail exactly what he must do: give Dreyfus a powerful sedative by hypodermic injection, send the staff on a wild-goose chase for plenty of hot water, somehow find Professor Fassbender and his daughter, get them out of the castle, then take Dreyfus into custody. Clouseau estimated the entire operation would take approximately ten minutes.

"Hurry, Doctor." Dreyfus was making it easy for his rival. "I am in agony."

Clouseau filled the hypodermic with enough sedation to knock out a horse, then doubled the prescription just to be on the safe side. He turned to face

Dreyfus, the hypodermic held at a jaunty angle. "Roll up your sleeve," Clouseau ordered.

At sight of the needle, cold perspiration broke out on Dreyfus's brow. "No needle," he insisted. And no amount of persuasion could change his mind.

"But it makes only a small hole," Clouseau tried to explain. "See?" Clouseau jabbed the nedle into his own arm to demonstrate, gritting his teeth to stifle a cry of pain. Several drops of the sedative dribbled into Clouseau's bloodstream. Realizing what he had done, he yanked the needle out.

Clouseau began to stall for time. Seconds ticked away. Odd, but he found himself yawning. He shook his head, clearing it. So, he reasoned, the hypodermic-needle ploy had failed. Fortunately, he still had plenty of tricks up his sleeve.

"Shouldn't I go and get some hot water for you?" It was Hindu Harry trying to be helpful.

"Of course not," Clouseau replied. "If you wish to be helpful, why don't you go and get me some hot water?"

Cairo Fred opened the door as Hindu Harry hurried out of the room. "You, too," Clouseau commanded Cairo Fred. "I always require lots of hot water when I work. It helps to wash up the blood."

Cairo Fred hesitated and looked toward Dreyfus. "Do what the doctor says," Dreyfus mumbled.

"And be sure to lock the door," Clouseau called. "I do not like to be interrupted." He leaned over Dreyfus. "Open wide." Dreyfus complied. "Wider." Clouseau looked into the patient's mouth. Dreyfus had practically unhinged his jaws.

"Mmmmm," said Clouseau knowingly, and pursed his lips. Dreyfus waited nervously.

"Is that a good 'mmmmm' or a bad 'mmmmm'?" the patient asked.

"That all depends." Clouseau was proud of the way he was managing to carry off the deception.

"Depends on what?" Dreyfus persisted. The man was becoming a nuisance.

"Whether you are for or against extraction," Clouseau replied. "Tell me, does this hurt?"

Clouseau picked up a small screwdriver and began tapping his way around the inside of Dreyfus's mouth, being mindful to strike all teeth along the way. On the twenty-second tooth Dreyfus roared in agony.

"That's the naughty one," the strange dentist explained. "Maybe I should make sure?" He lifted the screwdriver.

"No!" yelped Dreyfus. "One out of one is enough!" His eyes rolled as Clouseau picked up a wicked-looking pair of extractors. "Aren't you going to try to put in a filling?"

"With what?" The dentist smiled. "I couldn't fill that hole with my elbow! The tooth has got to come out. Otherwise you will be a cripple for life."

Dreyfus was too crazed with pain to question the logic of the statement. "You're the doctor, Doctor." He giggled. "Go ahead. I'll try to be brave. Only, couldn't you give me something to put me out?"

Clouseau yawned and looked about in confusion. "Out?" he asked. "Why on earth would I want to do that? I just arrived."

Dreyfus gnashed his teeth, which only served to increase the pain. "I can't stand much more of this," he cried. "Give me a painkiller, man! Knock me out! Only hurry!"

Clouseau looked about for a blunt instrument. On a nearby table lay an ancient mace. Clouseau picked it up. The mace was so heavy he was forced to use both hands. Clouseau put the mace behind his back and walked over to Dreyfus. "Close your eyes," he instructed. Dreyfus complied. Clouseau raised the mace over his head, staggered back under the weight of the weapon, and fell down a narrow flight of stairs he had failed to notice.

Dreyfus sat up and looked around for the dentist. For some odd reason he came walking up the stairs, scowling darkly. "Whoever designed this fool castle certainly knew very little about stair placement," he commented.

Something began nagging at Dreyfus. A dentist who fell down a flight of stairs in the middle of a consultation? Dreyfus tried to pursue the fleeing thought through waves of pain.

"I was preoccupied with the anesthetic," the dentist was explaining. "Now I shall have to start all over. Sit down if you please."

Dreyfus obeyed and closed his eyes. Clouseau began rubbing his chin. To his horor he discovered the wax was beginning to melt. Hurriedly he looked into the doctor's little black bag for something—anything. He picked up a small can and read the label: "Nitrous Oxide." He failed to notice that below that, in smaller type, was "Laughing Gas." Clouseau uncapped the can and took a deep whiff. It nearly knocked him down.

Clouseau poured a liberal amount of the liquid onto a towel and clamped it over the face of Dreyfus. "A few whiffs of this and you won't feel a thing." He giggled. Cairo Fred hammered on the door. "Hot water, Doc!" he yelled. "Open up!"

Clouseau found that hilarious. He walked over to the door, chuckling, and unlocked it. Cairo Fred entered with pails of hot water and a load of freshly laundered towels over his shoulder. "Put them down," the dentist suggested, "anywhere." He returned to his patient and dribbled a few more drops of nitrous oxide onto the cloth covering his face. "Breathe deeply," the dentist said laughing as Cairo Fred stared in amazement.

"What do you think I'm doing?" Dreyfus snickered. The patient went off into gales of mirth, wheezing and slapping his thigh.

Cairo Fred looked at them as though they were mad. "I've heard of painless dentistry . . ." he began.

Dreyfus pawed at the face covering. He saw the dentist peering down at him. Dreyfus thought the odd-looking doctor was the funniest thing he had ever seen. He laughed up into the doctor's face.

"See here," the dentist said, chuckling, "what is so funny?"

"I don't know!" Tears ran out of the corners of Dr. Dreyfus's eyes. He was laughing so hard his sides hurt.

The dentist brandished the extractors. He tittered, "Would you like me to pull your tooth now?"

"Ready any time you are, C. B.," quipped the patient and then laughed uproariously at his own witticism.

"I don't get it," the dentist wheezed.

Dreyfus pointed at the offending tooth toward the back of his upper jaw. "That's the one to get," he ordered.

"This may hurt." The dentist whooped. Peals of laughter rang out in the room. Hindu Harry thought his eardrums would burst.

"My pleasure!" shrieked Dreyfus.

Clouseau shoved the extractors into his patient's mouth and felt around for a tooth. Any tooth. He clamped the extractors together and pulled. Laughter had made him weak. He tried again, this time laughing harder. Dreyfus rolled back and forth in the chair, helpless with mirth. Clouseau collapsed on top of him, got a knee on Dreyfus's chest, and gave a mighty heave. The extractor came out holding a tooth. Clouseau giggled. Dreyfus looked at his tooth and started to laugh again.

"I don't know what you gave me, Doctor," he roared in a sudden paroxysm, "but I'm hallucinating! Your whole face is melting!"

Clouseau sobered fast. He rushed to the mirror and surveyed his likeness. Horrors! There was a decided list to his chin! Worse, his left brow had begun to slide into the eye socket. The effect gave Clouseau's contenance a look of utter depravity that some women might have found attractive. Working frantically and surreptitiously, Clouseau tried to reshape his features and merely managed to make himself appear more grotesque.

Hindu Harry rushed into the room. One look at his face would have given the impression that the end of the world had come.

"What is it?" Dreyfus was still laughing, unable to stop.

"We just got word," Hindu Harry reported. Clouseau is still alive!"

Peals of laughter shook Dreyfus. "I knew it!" he shrieked. Dreyfus pulled himself out of his chair and staggered over to the mirror. He opened his mouth and looked hard at his reflection. A front tooth on his jaw was missing. The dentist nudged him with his elbow, saw what he was looking at, and broke up.

"There is only one man in the entire world who would pull the wrong tooth!" Dreyfus screamed.

Clouseau giggled and nodded. Dreyfus waved feebly toward Cairo Fred. "Don't let him get away," he said indicating the dentist. Cairo Fred and Hindu Harry looked at each other in confusion as the dentist, driven to his knees by waves of laughter, managed to make his way to the door and out.

"You mean the dentist, Boss?" Cairo Fred summoned the courage to ask.

"Dentist my ass!" shouted Dreyfus. "It's Clouseau!" A key turned in the lock on the far side of the door. "Kill him!"

22

Clouseau leaned against the other side of the locked door. Gradually his laughter subsided and with it his drowsiness. He experienced such a wave of confidence he almost felt dizzy. His head clearing rapidly, Clouseau slipped down the long dank corridor, past the framed portraits of Mondscheins long dead. By God, Clouseau noticed as he looked about for an escape route, they were a homely group! "Handsome Harry" Mondschein, the pick of the litter, a dashing sixteenth-century cavalier, either had lived with a case of extreme acne or else mildew in the damp castle was causing his portrait to deteriorate.

From inside the impromptu dentist's office shots rang out, shattering the door lock. Cairo Fred and Hindu Harry charged out into the hall just as Clouseau ducked around a corner. The Indian and the Egyptian ran back to Dreyfus, who stood ranting and raving through the thick towel he held stuffed into his mouth.

"Ernglub glagg bnrnr!" screamed the infuriated Dreyfus. "At once!"

"Sure, Boss," Cairo Fred said placatingly. Dreyfus tore the towel from his bleeding mouth. "And don't patronize me, you moron!"

Hindu Harry nudged his partner. "What's 'patronize'?" he whispered. Before Cairo Fred could display his ignorance, Dreyfus hurled the bloody towel at him.

"I said bring Fassbender and his daughter to the war room without further delay or I shall have your ears for breakfast!"

Hindu Harry and Cairo Fred rushed out after Clouseau. "I guess now I know what patronize means," Hindu Harry confided. "Nice to be working for such an educated bastard, ain't it?"

Clouseau ran through a low wooden door and along a kind of catwalk that led onto a parapet. Suddenly he found himself racing across the ramparts of the castle. A plane flew overhead. Clouseau paused to watch and saw a line of twenty Egyptian paratroopers bail out, saw three chutes blossom, then counted seventeen fresh craters in the soft soil of the mountain meadow.

"Undoubtedly," Clouseau made a mental note, "in Cairo this maneuver will be considered an outstanding success." He heard footsteps coming and ran to a low wall, which in the past had been used to shield archers. Clouseau hopped over the wall and onto a tiny balcony overlooking the river. For a moment, if he did not lose his balance, he was safe. Clouseau reminded himself at all costs not to look down. "If you do, you are a gone goose."

Closeau looked down and almost lost his balance in shocked surprise at what he saw. A Soviet tank with a red star on its turret came trundling out of the forest pursued by a maddened, lust-crazed boar, which now began to attack the tank. The tank came to a stop on the far bank and trained its cannon on the drawbridge.

Two floors below, in the subservants' quarters, Cairo Fred unlocked the door of the small room inside which mugger Bruce the Knife sat guarding Professor Fassbender and his daughter. Not one to waste time, Bruce was practicing his trade on Margo, who did not seem too annoyed by the attention.

"Upstairs." Cairo Fred nudged the Professor with the barrel of his rifle. "Both of you."

Bruce demurred. "Can't you wait till I'm through?" Cairo Fred shook his head.

"Dreyfus is in a foul mood . . . even for him," he reported. Bruce pretended a sudden need to visit the bathroom, since he was a highly suspicious person who considered it extremely unlucky to be around crazy French ex-policemen.

Cairo Fred led the Fassbenders through the labyrinthine underground passages of the castle. As he passed the weapons room, he failed to notice Clouseau crossing the corridor directly behind him.

Clouseau sized up the situation in a flash. He started to run forward silently on his toes, tripped over a bearskin rug, and crashed into Cairo Fred, throwing him off balance. "I beg your pardon," Clouseau apologized, whereupon Cairo Fred picked him up and threw him against the opposite wall and into a display of yeoman's bows and arrows. Margo Fassbender promptly kicked Cairo Fred in the jaw, knocking him colder than a salmon. The Professor regarded his little girl with newfound respect.

"I'm a veritable hellcat when aroused," Margo panted. "That was fun! I wish the swarthy little shit would come-to so I could kick him again."

"That will not be necessary, my adorable little hellcat," Clouseau admonished as he picked up Fred's gun. He bent over the unconscious killer. "It's a good thing I decided only to render you unconscious," he told the man from Cairo.

The Professor stared at Clouseau, who instantly read the question in the scholar's eyes. "Allow me to introduce myself." Clouseau bowed, hitting his head on a carved table. "I am Chief Inspector Jacques Clouseau and I am here to assist you in escaping from this abominable castle. Now, if you will please follow me?"

Margo threw her arms around Clouseau's neck. "Thank God," she cried, "We're saved."

"Not yet," Clouseau cautioned. "And I would appreciate it if you were grateful later."

Clouseau placed a finger to his lips and motioned for the Fassbenders to follow him. The Professor hung back. "You take the girl," he said bravely. "I have to stop Dreyfus."

Margo dug her fingers into Clouseau's arm, making him wince. "Please," she begged. "Don't let him! Can't you see? He means to sabotage the Doomsday Machine!"

"What washing machine?" Clouseau stared at the girl as though she were a raving lunatic.

Professor Fassbender gently placed Margo's hand in Clouseau's with the admonition to "take care of her, old man." The scientist turned to his daughter. "Don't you see, darling, that it must be done? And that I am the only one who can do it? Now, please be brave and go with the Inspector."

"*Chief* Inspector," corrected Clouseau. "Where did you say this Dummybaby Machine is?"

"In the laboratory," said Fassbender. "Why do you ask?"

"I ask," replied Clouseau, "for the simple reason that I cannot leave Mondschein Castle until I have apprehended the madman Dreyfus. Since you wish to sabotage this Monday Machine, I think I know a way to kill two stones with one bird." He paused. "Now, which way to the laboratory?"

Even as Clouseau spoke, Dreyfus was removing the protective, lead-sheeted tarpaulin from the Doomsday Machine. He sang as he worked.

Dreyfus got the cover off and then moved to a large map of England pinned to the wall. He checked the latitude and longitude for London, did some quick figuring with a slide rule, and began to activate the focus mechanism of the Doomsday Machine. Before he could finish, the door flew open. Dreyfus whirled and stared into the face of his nemesis, Chief Inspector Clouseau. For some reason Dreyfus could not fathom, the pilot was dressed in Cairo Fred's clothes and carried his automatic. Dr. Fassbender and Margo were with Clouseau, whom Dreyfus rudely ignored.

"Ah, Professor," said Dreyfus cordially. "You are just in time to help me select a target for our little toy." He patted the Doomsday Machine affectionately. "The British betrayed me, so they must pay. Now . . . what shall I destroy? Buckingham Palace?" Dreyfus shook his head. "Too small. How about London? But why stop there? Why not England herself?"

Clouseau decided the time to act had come. He cleared his throat and stepped forward. "Paul Dreyfus, common criminal, it is my unpleasant duty to arrest you in the name of the law."

Behind Clouseau and out of his sight, Hindu Harry walked into the laboratory holding a submachine gun. "Drop it, Frenchy!" he said laconically. Hindu Harry loved American Westerns and knew that the bad guys always spoke in that fashion.

Clouseau whirled. "Who are you calling 'Frenchy'?" he demanded. Clouseau caught sight of the submachine gun pointed at his navel. "You see? Frenchy is happy to drop it," he said dropping the automatic to the floor. Dreyfus beamed at Hindu Harry, who was momentarily confused by the unexpected expression of favor from the terrible Dreyfus. Margo took advantage of the distraction. As Hindu Harry bent to pick up the gun, she kicked him in the jaw. Across the laboratory, Professor Fassbender broke the computer bank.

"No! No!" screamed Dreyfus. "Stop him!"

"Why should we do that?" Clouseau picked up the submachine gun. "Nobody here is on your side!" Suddenly, the submachine gun in Clouseau's hands began firing ugly bursts. Dreyfus dove for cover. Hindu Harry sat up, saw what was happening, and fainted. Margo hopped up and down and yelled "Shoot them!" while her father pushed buttons and reset computer dials hurriedly.

The shooting stopped. Clouseau checked the submachine gun. "I seem to be out of bullets," he observed as Dreyfus jumped him.

"Get out!" shouted Dr. Fassbender. "You have five minutes to save yourself!"

Clouseau struggled with the maddened Dreyfus. "How can I save myself when this crazy person is biting me on the neck?" Clouseau asked. "Eh? Can you answer me that?"

Dreyfus removed his fangs from Clouseau's neck and stared at Fassbender. "You're bluffing," he accused. In his heart he knew he was not. The Professor looked too self-satisfied.

"Look at the computer," invited the world-celebrated scientist. Everyone stared at the computer bank. It appeared to be running wild, completely out of control. The wrong lights flashed as incorrect formulae continued feeding themselves into the machine's memory bank. A circuit breaker malfunctioned. Then an entire relay system blew out. On its platform the Doomsday Machine started to revolve. The deadly needle nose retracted and then depressed until it was aimed directly into the laboratory.

"No! Stop it! You're ruining me!" Dreyfus was unraveling like a worn-out tennis sweater.

"It's took late." The Professor smiled the small, brave smile of a man about to see his life's work go up in smoke. "Nothing can stop it now."

Hindu Harry broke for the door as smoke began pouring from the nearest generator. Alarm signals were activated. "Danger" signs began flashing. Hearing the commotion, Cairo Fred and Bruce the Knife rushed into the castle courtyard and frantically began lowering the drawbridge.

Dreyfus saw his dreams beginning to collapse around him. "It's not fair!" He stamped his foot and began to cry like a spoiled child.

Clouseau turned toward the laboratory door. "After you," he said gallantly.

"You first," the Professor insisted. Clouseau remained adamant. Margo glared her displeasure.

"Will one of you jerks get his ass the hell out of here before I get angry?" she called out. "You seem to forget I'm a hellcat when aroused."

Clouseau and the Professor simultaneously moved toward the door, jamming themselves in the narrow doorframe. "I can't move," Clouseau said. "Neither can I," the Professor discovered. It was Margo who broke the log jam. She kicked Clouseau in the rear, spinning him out through the doorway like a cork from a bottle of champagne. Margo ran after him, followed by the Professor. They raced through deserted rooms and salons, down corridors filled with fleeing servants, some of whom began leaping out of windows into the millstream below. The walls of Mondschein Castle began to glow and shimmer.

In the great hall the Professor came to a sudden stop beside the massive Wurlitzer. "I'm going back for Dreyfus," he announced. "You two go on. We'll meet on the far and distant shore."

Margo cried out. "Daddy! No!"

Professor Fassbender took his daughter's tear-stained face in his hands and kissed it tenderly. "I can't be the cause of another man's death," he said quietly. "Why, when I was a boy I couldn't even pull the wings off butterflies. You go on. I'll make it."

The Professor turned and bravely started retracing his steps toward where certain death waited in the laboratory. Margo broke away from Clouseau and ran after her father. Clouseau caught up with her, spun her around. Margo kicked Clouseau in the jaw. He fell like a stone. Margo looked at her shoe. "Not bad," she mused. "Three for three."

Now there was no time to go after her father and Margo knew it. She picked up Clouseau in a fireman's carry and started running for the drawbridge.

Across the river, soldiers began to emerge from the woods. They stood along the bank and stared at what was beginning to happen to Mondschein Castle. Wisps of smoke began drifting up from the turrets. A lacy spire burst into puce-colored flame that gave off a strange, chemical odor.

Greek troops stood beside Turkish cavalrymen, their ancient animosities forgotten in this Götterdämmerung. Members of the Japanese Attack Team began to run around taking pictures. A tall Irish corporal lifted a short British lieutenant onto his shoulders, where he could see better. Members of a Ecuadorean antitank crew shared their tuna-fish sandwiches with a couple of Californians. A Syrian fighter pilot put down his bottle of Manischewitz as organ music began to peal from deep inside the doomed castle.

Dreyfus was seated at his beloved Wurlitzer, playing as he had never played before, lost in a reverie of total bliss. A beatific smile lit his features. Dreyfus played and sang all of the tunes he loved best: "The Party's Over," "This Is the End of a Beautiful Friendship," "Moon Over Miami." He was segueing from "Melancholy Baby" to "It's a Grand Night for Singing" when Dr. Fassbender stalked into the room, his face streaked with smoke.

Outside the castle, Margo carried Clouseau across the drawbridge and there were tears in her eyes.

"Man, that sumbitch can really play," noted a lance corporal in the uniform of a South African regiment. The Bantu standing beside him nodded in agreement.

Eyes closed, Dreyfus continued to play. When Fassbender spoke to him, it was as though the other did not hear. Fassbender tapped Dreyfus gently on the shoulder. Dreyfus opened his eyes, smiling. "Any last requests?" he asked.

"Come with me," pleaded Professor Fassbender. "You can still make it."

Dreyfus let his fingers wander over the banks of keys. "How About 'Beat Me Daddy Eight to the Bar'?" he asked. "Or 'Moon River' or 'Come on-a My House'?"

Fassbender lifted Dreyfus's fingers and tried to lead him away. Dreyfus hooked his feet under the organ stool, so that it was impossible to budge him. "Save yourself, Professor," he said quietly. "I prefer to go down with my castle."

The Professor did a surprising thing. He sat down beside Dreyfus. They began to play a four-handed arrangement of "Kitten on the Keys" in perfect harmony. Neither of them noticed when the vaulted ceiling began to fall in.

That night, in describing the last moments of the stricken castle the Evening News quoted an eyewitness paramedic from Abilene: "That danged place looked like a big ole jukebox blowin' up."

Sparks shot up hundreds of feet into the sky. Choking puce-colored smoke drifted across the river and into the Gruppenwald Forest, where leaves fell like so many tears and rabbits ran around in a frenzy, biting their own tails. The walls of Mondschein Castle bulged outward, then sagged and collapsed inward. The great roof and belfry toppled over as a high, electronic sound whined through the valley.

The sun hid behind a cloud bank. When it reappeared seconds later, nothing remained of Mondschein

Castle. Not a trace of foundation or drawbridge. Not so much as a scorched outline around the perimeter to show where the feared and mighty castle had once stood.

23

The black police Citroën pulled up smartly before Clouseau's apartment house. François hurried around from the driver's side and opened the door for his chief. Clouseau was in an expansive mood, as befits a man who once again had written his name into the criminologist's Valhalla alongside those of Nick and Nora Charles, Peter Gunn, and Inspector Maigret.

"It has been quite a day," Clouseau murmured. He flicked a dust particle from the new decoration in his lapel.

"Again, my congratualtions." François bowed.

"Por nada," Clouseau replied. "That is Spanish," he confided. "I am broadening my horizons. I suggest that you do the same." Poor confused François nodded. Clouseau smiled. "Until tomorrow."

François gunned the Citroën away from the curb, in the process splashing Clouseau with gutter water.

The great detective let himself into his apartment, humming. "Cato?" he called. "Come, my little yellow friend and hang up my coat for me, there's the good wog." There was no sound. The flat seemed to be deserted.

Clouseau softly shut the door and fell into his karate crouch. Stealthily, he made his way down the hall, ready to deal with instant attack. But this time Cato had chosen his ambush well.

Clouseau stepped into the bedroom and dropped his hands in astonishment. The room was bare. Under Clouseau's spare trench coat, which he usually kept in the closet in case of emergency, so was Lena Berriossiva.

"I hope you do not mind," she crooned lewdly, "But I gave Cato the night off."

Clouseau shrugged. "I do not mind. What I do mind is that while I was involved in the never-ending war against crime, some swine came in and carted off all my furniture."

Lena laughed a tiny, nymphomaniacal laugh that raised Clouseau's hackles. "Forgive me, darling, but I took the liberty of redecorating your bedroom."

Lena shrugged out of the trench coat and pushed a tiny button on the wall. The lights went from bright to dim to erotic. Music throbbed from the quadriphonic sound system that had been cleverly built into the bidet in the adjoining bathroom. As Clouseau stood transfixed, the far wall turned slowly on concealed casters and hinges until it was horizontal and had become a superkingsize bed. Lena stepped up onto the huge water bed and began bouncing up and down seductively. "Well?" she invited. "What are you standing there for, you big lug?"

Clouseau did not need to be asked twice. He tore off his clothes, breaking the band of the wristwatch the Mayor of Paris had given him personally only that morning. Clouseau flung himself upon the willing Lena.

"My darling!" he cried.

"Dear heart," called Lena in a voice husky with passion.

"Aiyeeeeee!" screamed Cato as he launched himself onto his master from inside the record player.

Under Cato's impact, the bed's retracting mechanism was activated. The bed snapped back up into the wall, carrying its occupants with it.

A startled gendarme walking his beat outside swore that he saw the outside wall of Clouseau's apartment building burst open under terrific impact, which sent Hero, Heroine, and Faithful Manservant hurtling ass over teakettle into the Seine, where they were rescued two miles downstream.

To reach the Ultimate Galaxy of the recently discovered Dimension Quattro, it is necessary to turn left at the Milky Way and then to proceed due east by northeast for several trillions of light-years. A traveler making the journey from planet Earth would, if he embarked on his travel through space at age twenty-five, be exactly one million six hundred and fifty-nine thousand three hundred and nineteen years old, not counting leap years, by the time he arrived.

Through an infinite plain, beautiful in the purity of its emptiness, strolled Professor Fassbender and former Chief Inspector Dreyfus. They were evidently deep in thought, having just taken lunch in the cafeteria of the United Nations Building, which was just visible on the seventh gradient of the horizon. Actually the two men were glad to have the cafeteria, since it was the only restaurant in the galaxy.

Normally, Fassbender and Dreyfus amused themselves after a meal by going into the vast emptiness of the General Assembly chamber and sailing paper airplanes made from old NATO agreements at one another. But today was different. Fassbender somehow sensed that Dreyfus finally wanted to get something off his chest.

"Well, Professor," said the Frenchman, probing for an opening, "like it or not, you appear to be stuck with a madman."

Fassbender, who was more of a philosopher, disagreed. "I would say," he corrected, "that we're stuck with each other. Besides, up here you don't seem to be the least bit mad."

They walked in silence while Dreyfus thought about it. "As a matter of fact, I haven't felt the same since the day before Clouseau joined the Sûreté." He smiled happily as he said this, and then began humming a little far-out tune that he made up on the spot.

"I wonder," said Professor Fassbender. "Do you play chess?"

"Yes," answered Dreyfus, and added eagerly, "Do you play canasta?" When Fassbender confessed that he had never learned, Dreyfus, in a rare outburst of camaraderie, promised to teach him—provided they could come up with playing cards.

Somewhere the barking of a dog suddenly shattered the astral quiet. The men reacted in astonishment as the upper half of the French poodle, Shlep, frolicked across the starscape and bounded up to them on its front legs. Shlep expressed his joy at finding human companionship by wiggling his ears, since his tail, along with his lower extremities, was back on earth.

"It is a mutant?" the Professor eyed Shlep nervously. Dreyfus laughed. He explained it was the dog that had been miraculously sliced in half by the Doomsday Machine laser that removed the UN Building on a long-forgotten October thirtieth many years ago.

The Professor studied the half of Shlep that was present. His scientist's mind was racing. "If I could get the separate halves of the dog into the same time dimension," he speculated, "some sort of fusion might take place." He looked at Dreyfus. "What do you think?"

"You're the doctor." Dreyfus chuckled, then stopped as an alarming thought entered his consciousness. "You're not thinking of going back for anything," he said anxiously. "I tell you, I wouldn't go back to Earth if they paved the Champs Élysées with Clouseau clones!"

In Fassbender's eyes the flames of inspiration quickly died. He relaxed. "It was just a thought," he explained. "A wild thought. From another experience. What is important from now on is how the three of us—correction, the two and a half of us—are going to learn to live in peace with one another."

"Don't worry," Dreyfus reassured Dr. Fassbender. "We will."

"But are you sure?" the scientist took off his shoe and threw it far out toward the horizon for Shlep to fetch.

"I'm sure," Dreyfus said, a slight edge coming into his voice.

"If only we could be sure," the Professor muttered. "If only we could make some sort of a meaningful beginning."

Dreyfus glared at the humanoid walking beside him. "Professor," he warned, "you're starting to bug me."